KU-215-334

PENGUIN BOOKS

THE BIRDS OF THE AIR

Alice Thomas Ellis was born in Liverpool before the war and was educated at Bangor Grammar School and Liverpool School of Art. She has written five novels to date: *The Sin Eater* (1977), which received a Welsh Arts Council Award for 'a book of exceptional merit'; *The Birds of the Air* (1980, Penguin 1983), which also won a Welsh Arts Council Award; *The 27th Kingdom* (Penguin 1982), which was nominated for the Booker Prize in 1982; *The Other Side of the Fire* (Penguin 1985); and *Unexplained Laughter* (Penguin 1986).

Under her married name (Anna Haycraft) she has written two cookery books, *Natural Baby Food* and, with Caroline Blackwood, *Darling, You Shouldn't Have Gone to So Much Trouble* (1980).

She is married to Colin Haycraft, chairman and managing director of Duckworth publishers, of which she is a director and the fiction editor. They have five children.

Alice Thomas Ellis

THE BIRDS
OF THE AIR

PENGUIN BOOKS

Penguin Books Ltd, Harmondsworth, Middlesex, England
Viking Penguin Inc., 40 West 23rd Street, New York, New York 10010, U.S.A.
Penguin Books Australia Ltd, Ringwood, Victoria, Australia
Penguin Books Canada Limited, 2801 John Street, Markham, Ontario, Canada L3R 1B4
Penguin Books (N.Z.) Ltd, 182–190 Wairau Road, Auckland 10, New Zealand

First published by Gerald Duckworth & Co. Ltd 1980
Published in Penguin Books 1983
Reprinted 1987

Made and printed in Great Britain by
Richard Clay (The Chaucer Press) Ltd, Bungay, Suffolk

TO JOSHUA

All his beauty, wit and grace
Lie forever in one place.
He who sang and sprang and moved
Now, in death, is only loved.

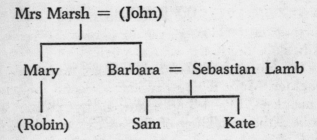

'IT'S GOING TO SNOW for Christmas,' called Mrs Marsh from the kitchen, raising her voice – unnecessarily since the house was so small.

The tone of cheerful kindliness annoyed her daughter. Mary felt rather like someone for whom a marriage was being arranged by people who doubted the suitability of the match but who could think of no seemly way of retiring. Her family and friends behaved like outsiders privy to a secret and dubious courtship, treating her with an arch, considered and wholly unnatural care, whispering together and falling silent when they remembered her sitting by the window and possibly listening. She supposed she must be dying, and wondered whether, if she touched the window pane with her cold finger, the cold would seep in from outside as though by osmosis.

The wind had taken over the dark winter garden, growing wilder as the morning passed, rattling through the bluntly pruned twigs of the rose bushes, which clanked like an armoury, and arbitrarily redisposing the few remaining leaves of autumn, sweeping them past her gaze, lost and despairing – the unquiet dead taken by surprise.

No woman, well or ill, could sit in the garden today without looking foolish and feeling harried. The wind changed course, sycophantically smoothing the uprising mane of the cypresses and tearing away to flatten the common yellowed grasses that still stood, lifeless and fading, on the ridge.

Nor had the cat ventured out today. Most mornings he walked the ridge, describing his territory with a formal heraldic precision. A bold feral tom, striped like a flag, tail waving, he would stroll and lean and sway among the stalks, nose uplifted, sniffing, throat stretched, eyes half closed, absorbed and proud, the only thing to retain its fluidity, alive and warm and moving in the frozen grasses. Sometimes Mary sitting in the garden would hiss jealously from behind the philadelphus and watch him leap away startled, all selfhood lost in the indignity of fright.

Beyond the ridge, beyond the hollow, lay the old wolf-coloured woods, grizzled with snow: ground untouched by man, who could find no use for it. There would have been forest there when the Great Worm lay curled in the declivity, where now were raised neat and placid chimneys, and the Terrible Lizard moved along the cat's ridge, ambulant architecture, a saurian cathedral, the Creator's tribute to himself before he thought of making men to praise his genius. Mary raised her eyes higher to encompass her image of this reptile, vast and indifferent, confident beyond the need of pride, surveying the woods with his small eyes when the world was warm

8

– before Robin had lived or died. It was more pleasant to imagine the manless irrelevance of prehistory than to regret the recent comely countryside supplanted by dull suburb. It was painless to dream.

The wind sprang like a dog at the eucalyptus in the hedge and the leaves turned their pale backs to its bullying, shivering and pulling away. Mary sat by the window thinking of wilderness, of wastes of ice and sky, of the long wide light, cold beyond sensation or reflection. She hardly noticed the sparrows hopping and picking at the crazy paving just outside the window, where lay crumbs and bits of chopped bacon rind under a bush still carrying a crimson rose that had stayed too long and hung frozen and shamed on a bare branch.

What does she find to stare at all day, wondered Mrs Marsh irritably, shaking out a tablecloth on the lawn with more crumbs for the poor birds and observing her daughter, as so often now, close to the window and surely cold. She trotted into Mary's room folding the cloth.

'Is that a book you've got there?' she demanded.

'Yes,' conceded Mary.

'Then read it,' said her mother, dancing with exasperation, *read* it.'

*   *   *

Seventy-two miles away Sam stared at the window of his mother's drawing room, observing a fly that had dropped out of nowhere and appeared to be

9

drunk. It crawled along the ledge and suddenly rolled over on its back, waving its legs. Sam wondered whether the faint buzz he could hear was the fly giggling, or possibly weeping.

Outside this window lay the university town which Sam found unrewarding save for the bus station and the caff where the men from the motor works ate their meat-and-two-veg and drank their tea. He yawned. His mother had roused him at 10.30, whispering that his father was about and would soon be asking what the children were doing. 'Kate is tidying her room,' she added, gazing round in reproachful comparison. Sam had listened stoically. If it hadn't been for his sister he would have been a better boy. The urgent necessity not to resemble Kate in any way had led him into much trouble.

Barbara had spent the rest of the morning in the dining room wrapping up last-minute presents she had made herself for people who would have been glad to be spared the necessity of saying thank you: the college porter who had been so obliging one day, the charlady, some ex-*au pair* girls, a few half-dead old aunts – not Aunt Gwennie, she'd died.

Sam knew they would all have preferred bottles of booze or packets of fags anyway, but his mother said those things lacked the personal touch and went on packing pomanders and mittens and boxes of grainy fudge – hurrying and fumbling a little because some of Sebastian's undergraduates were coming in for drinks before lunch. These were the dregs left over at the end of term who had had to make special arrangements with their landladies, while their more fortunate or popular fellows had gone to their own, or each other's, loving homes or on skiing holidays.

Sam knew what they'd be like. His mother said they were *delightful* – which meant they'd be black, miner's children, acned or similarly disadvantaged. He felt sorry for them. They had probably come to this place with charming visions of themselves attired in college scarves, blazers and gowns, floating down-river on punts, clutching armfuls of dreaming spires. Though he couldn't understand their hopes and aspirations, he sympathised with their disappointment. And he pitied anyone forced into regular confrontation with his father in the role of teacher. His own experiences of this had left a deep, lasting and negative impression.

'Do find a book to read, Sam,' his mother said when she became aware of him lounging behind the chesterfield biting his nails, but Sam had set his face against the academic world and had determined on a career in sound equipment.

His little sister came in with her writing-pad and pencil. She was writing a book of verse and Sam wished her head would fall off.

'Mummy,' Kate asked. 'How do you spell "ephemeral"?'

His mother made a telephone call before the first student arrived. 'Ephemeral . . .' she was saying. 'Just imagine. Only a few days now, Mummy,' she concluded. 'All our love to Mary.'

'That was Barbara,' said Mrs Marsh, delighted with the news of Kate, her gifted grandchild. 'She sends her love.'

'I know,' said Mary absently.

'What do you mean, you *know*?' asked her mother, suddenly cross again.

'I mean she always does,' explained Mary.

'But how did you know who I was talking to?' persisted her mother.

'Extrasensory perception,' said Mary.

Mrs Marsh looked at her suspiciously. 'You're silly,' she accused; 'you heard me say "Barbara".' She glanced round the room hoping to catch something in the process of untidying itself. 'You haven't got enough coal on the fire,' she remarked, 'and you haven't got your cardigan on. I don't know why you don't have a nice clean electric fire.' She had forgotten that she had herself insisted on opening up the fireplace when it became clear that Mary could no longer live alone and must come to be cared for in her mother's neat, peaceful widow's house. 'So much more lively,' she had said courageously, 'so much more cheerful.' She knelt and swept up a scatter of ash with a little brass dustpan and brush, asking, 'What would you like for lunch?'

'Anything,' said Mary, aware that lunch was already prepared, and moving obediently to the chair by the fire.

Mrs Marsh hung her brush back on its tripod

and looked up. There was a swift winged dispute on the sylvan bird-table and she jumped to the window, flapping the curtain. 'These ones are doing it now,' she said bewilderedly. 'Last time I came back from the hospital over the downs all the birds were fighting.'

'They do,' said Mary. 'Especially robins.' She spoke that name with careful interest, as one in pain might move just to see how much pain there could be.

'Oh, not robins,' cried her mother, thinking of her Christmas cards before she remembered that Robin was dead. She liked the story of the robin who had tried to pluck the thorns from the crown of Jesus and soaked his little breast in red blood, and she couldn't suppress a feeling of annoyance with Mary's Robin for being dead. The event had upset her daughter out of all proportion. Of course it was a dreadful thing to lose your loved ones, but life had to go on. What would happen if everyone collapsed?

'That's why you never see more than one,' said Mary. 'He's slain all the others.'

'Don't be silly, dear,' said Mrs Marsh, who anyway had never cared for Mary's view of nature – of what precisely flowers were, and why birds sang. 'The poor little things are hungry, and it's made them bad-tempered. I'll get your lunch, pet,' she added, having taken to using endearments previously foreign to her. She didn't dare tell her daughter outright that she loved her, since Mary was ill and might be frightened. All overt expressions of affection had terminal connotations: statements of love came at

13

last moments – the ends of letters, farewells on railway stations, turning over to go to sleep.

Now Mary could no longer see the brief wilderness – only the garden, the wide border that in the summer shone with flowers, the shrub-enclosed lawn that stopped at one side in a rustic fence to support the sweet peas that would screen the vegetable plot, melancholy now with rimed bolted cabbage stalks and blackened stands of beans. The people of Innstead concealed their vegetable gardens, preferring to contemplate in season the useless glories of aster and delphinium, petunia and pelargonium, lobelia, lupin, chrysanthemum and mesembryanthemum.

The sky had darkened when Mrs Marsh came back with lunch. She pushed open the door with her bottom, balancing a tray covered with two cloths, one under and one over the food, lest germs should leap on it in the few feet between the kitchen and her child.

'Why didn't you turn the light on?' she asked, though if it had been on she would have asked why Mary hadn't called her to do it, or remarked that too much light was bad for the eyes. Life had so treated her in recent years that she couldn't trust it to itself for a second. A solitary magpie – vain, god-cursed bird, clad in its eternal half-mourning – flew forever across her mind's eye and had to be propitiated or cunningly foiled with constant changing and rearranging. By questioning and vigilance fate might be deflected.

She pulled up a small round table and unveiled

the tray with its lidded pot of tomato soup, lightly boiled egg hidden in a cosy, strips of toast ready buttered, banana and glass of water. The cosy was painstakingly embroidered to match the roses and forget-me-nots of the egg cup, as this was a district where the members of the Women's Institute were dainty rather than robust, embroiderers and flower-arrangers rather than makers of chutney and whole-grain bread.

'Or you could have an orange if you preferred?'

'This will be perfect, thank you,' said Mary, who though she didn't feel at all guilty about imposing on her mother tried to give as little actual trouble as possible.

'Won't it be nice when Barbara and Kate are here?' urged Mrs Marsh. 'And Sam and Sebastian too,' she added with less enthusiasm.

'Lovely,' agreed Mary.

'A family Christmas,' continued Mrs Marsh dreamily. 'All of us together.'

Later, at the kitchen sink, she convicted herself of tactlessness and, as punishment, washed the dishes in water that was slightly too hot for her little white hands, for assuredly had things been otherwise Mary would not have been here.

But I am coping very well, she thought, comparing herself with her daughter and torn between pride and pity. She missed John very badly. She permitted herself to weep a little each morning in the bathroom before she put on her eyeshadow, but she knew and accepted what apparently Mary did not – that life had to go on. Mary had gone far, but had been wounded and forced to return; and her mother felt the ever so slightly spiteful vindication of the keeper of the cage. The bird had come back, if only to die.

Mary was at the window again, watching the antics of the wind.

*   *   *

Sam was eating a bowlful of peanuts and some pickled gherkins. He had hidden half a bottle of sherry under the valance of the chesterfield, and he sipped from it when he was sure he was unobserved.

On the chesterfield sat two undergraduates: a Ghanaian who couldn't afford the fare home and a lad from a northern grammar school in similar straits. This lad, after a while – perhaps to show his lack of prejudice, perhaps because he resented the relentless hospitality to which he was being subjected, or perhaps simply because, like most people, he disliked Sebastian Lamb – had a further fatal sherry and remarked, 'Old Lamb looks shagged out. He probably spent the morning screwing the Thrush.'

Their gruff, knowing laughter had thinned slightly as they shifted and descried Sam in his hiding-place behind them. One, at least, had paled a little, realising too late that this was indiscretion.

'Screwing the Thrush,' Sam had repeated to himself musingly throughout the afternoon. 'Screwing the Thrush . . .' Round about tea time he had remembered that the Thrush was what they called the wife

16

of the Professor of Music, and he had blushed until he thought his skin must shrivel.

'Move away from that radiator,' his mother advised. 'Or take off your sweater. Drink your tea.'

* * *

'Another cup?' asked Mrs Marsh, glancing with disfavour at the now ebony-gleaming windows. '*Anyone* could see in,' she complained.

'Not a great many people frequent other people's gardens,' said Mary, wary of curtains – for what if tonight should become the day of resurrection and Robin stand unseen in the garden? *Dies irae*.

'Dennis does,' said her mother, speaking of the retired police officer who lived next door. 'He's always creeping round people's gardens.'

'Dennis is crazy,' said Mary.

Well, perhaps he *was* a little, thought Mrs Marsh. Dennis had nothing to do and she knew he missed her husband. John had been kind to him with his unchanging warm politeness so unlike the chilly manners of the other people in the Close. But she never let herself think too long of her dead husband, for that way lay resentment and depression.

'Ah well,' she said, pouring the tea into two copiously floral cups. 'Do you remember the teas Mrs Lewis used to give us at Melys y Bwyd?' she asked after a while, her memory stirred by the wild flowers stitched into the tray-cloth.

'No,' lied Mary.

'They were lovely,' lied her mother.

She had been so happy with John and her two little girls, holidaying, content in the high-hedged, stone-walled cottage safely away from traffic and the mad rapist. The tractor and the village idiot had worried her not at all – nor even the farm cockerel and the road-lumbering cows on their way to be milked in the reassuring presence of the farmer and his boy. Like everyone else, she had transferred her atavistic terror of the woods and wilderness to the city. Great Pan had left the deserted places, put on black face and gone into the streets to become a mugger. The fearful desolation of the tower block had supervened upon the awful terror of the grove. It was to the country that people now went to seek the safety that they would once have found in the company of their fellows. People who double-locked and chained the doors of their town houses slept contentedly in fields in open tents.

'You loved them,' claimed Mrs Marsh, misled by her daughter's protestations of forgetfulness. Her little girls had been so sweet in their summer frocks, walking up the lane to a Sunday farmhouse tea, believing her answers to their every question. 'It will be strawberry jam for tea and homemade cake,' she had told them; and 'That little white flower is called coltsfoot'; and 'It will be perfectly all right. Its mummy will come and take it back to the nest and make it better.'

Wandering fondly down this memory lane she came to a sudden halt – even recollection shadowed and chilled by the black yews that crouched enormously in the churchyard. Robin, she thought angrily. It was so difficult to remember the sequence of events – she must be getting old. She glanced guiltily at Mary, but her daughter looked perfectly composed, eating bread and butter.

Mary remembered the lane, pretty as a wedding, when she was a child: great laces and nets of umbels flung joyously down, meadowsweet and cow parsley; the wind whispering sentimentally on the crisp bosom of the blackthorn and sighing through the handkerchief-scented grasses; wild roses every shade of bridesmaid from riotous, hoydenish pink to the frailest nervous pallor; the matronly mother-of-the-groom purple of foxgloves; the urchin trails of ragged robin; something borrowed in the straying rape, something blue in the garter button of speedwell; new leaves, old trees ranged like solemn guests, and blown petals floating in the dark puddles.

It was a long time ago. Since then, down that wedding lane, dazed with summer, Robin had come, borne in a slow black hearse sorrowful with dying wreaths – Robin passive beyond understanding, disguised as stone. Stone-faced, calm, closed and cold; marbled with dissolution and grave with the gravity of earth, all flowering ceased.

How brave I was, thought Mary derisively – consoling those who loved me, for my loss. You must never let the bugger think he's got the upper hand, she had told them, speaking of Death, and burning with crazy joy like a torture victim who must feel something and can only feel pain. She had carried a carnation which a friend had stolen from the wreath of someone else, recently interred, to enliven her blackness and cheer her up. She had bent each of its little knees the length of its stem so that it genuflected while the words went on and the holy water was sprinkled. She still had it – brown and flattened between the pages of her missal.

'You caught a chill at that funeral,' accused her mother, growing crosser and abandoning the pretence that neither knew what the other was thinking.

'It was eighty in the shade,' said Mary.

'Why you had to have a funeral in the country . . .' her mother was saying. 'Father's buried here . . . all that way . . . so tiring . . .' Mrs Marsh had imagined for a while that bereavement would change Mary, that Mary would now understand her and grow closer, but Mary had burned, as remote as a salamander in a blazing exaltation of grief, seeming to draw energy from what should have devoured her, and when she emerged she had, it is true, changed, but she was no closer.

'A waste of money,' concluded Mrs Marsh. She looked almost with dislike at the strange woman in whom her little daughter was now subsumed. Not for the first time she mourned that daughter as though she were already dead.

'Put your cardigan on,' she said. She took the tea things out – a bright, cross little woman, brave as an officer. 'Supper soon,' she promised.

* * *

That night Barbara gave a party – a real one this time, for Sebastian's colleagues.

'Come in,' she cried encouragingly, as the first guest arrived. 'How lovely to see you!'

Sam scowled. His mother saw that woman nearly every day. It couldn't always be lovely.

'Professor . . .' she said, 'let me take your coat. Katherine, do you know . . . ? Sam, find Sir Albert a drink. Now Elizabeth, what will you have? Mrs Potts, you were able to come! How lovely . . .'

Yak yak yak, thought Sam sourly. He slopped some white wine into a glass and handed it to a professor, who didn't want it and looked round aggrievedly for the whisky.

The rooms were filling up with academics quite quickly now: straight dull dons, though not many; old creamy dons, mannered as mandarins; a poor don twitching with paranoia; a rich don, unctuous as mayonnaise; sad neurotic dons; and one or two who were possibly clinically insane. There were ladies dressed in their best who looked as though they'd been moulded out of short squat boxes; dons' wives, earnest and helpful, or etiolated in their husbands' shade and thrusting out eagerly, desperately, for a little light; some wives of heads of houses, incandescent with confidence and as bossy as Dr Johnson; and one or two dons' husbands. They reminded Sam of his late peers at Mrs Bright's nursery school, to which all the university toddlers were despatched to

21

be set off on the right foot. It would have been futile to deny that jealousy, ill-will and ambition were powerfully present; but just as Mrs Bright's firm and kindly eye kept the kiddies in check, so ancient usage and the edicts of extreme refinement kept the university from outright shows of pride and hostility. In this ordered atmosphere dangerous emotions were allowed measured expression and all was secure.

'Sam,' said his mother. 'Darling, why don't you take the girls upstairs and play them your records?'

Sam regarded the girls. Although older, they resembled Kate, ugly and obedient and eager to do as their parents wished. He turned away.

'Sam,' insisted his mother tentatively. She was nervous. Sam had refused to change out of his torn jeans, leather jacket and tennis shoes. The ensuing altercation had left her trembling and tearful. It emerged that he had swapped his Harris tweed jacket for the dreadful thing he was now wearing, and when she had expostulated about the expense he told her with quiet satisfaction that the leather jacket had been twice the price of the tweed one. 'S'a bargin,' he said, and Barbara had been forced to notice, yet again, that her world and her values were threatened by madness. 'You look like a yob,' she had told him hopelessly, and Sam had been offended. Later she wondered, puzzledly, why he hadn't been pleased.

Two lady philosophers had also turned up in tennis shoes, but this was no consolation to Barbara. They had proved themselves and were entitled to dress as they wished.

22

Barbara urged herself not to worry and put out a hand to a solitary female in petrol blue.

'Sam is such an original boy,' she confided to this person, who didn't care either way. 'A little trouble finding his feet,' she continued, and stopped as the guest, eyes glazing, turned to talk to someone more interesting.

Barbara turned too. After all, she knew everyone here. They were her friends.

'Margaret, how lovely to see you! We weren't sure you were back.' Determinedly she addressed herself to the distinguished anthropologist. 'You must find it so cold. Have an olive.'

In spite of herself she stretched her neck sideways to see what Sam was doing now. She could just see the top of his head above the chesterfield. He'd be biting his nails, or picking his nose. He wasn't a sociable boy. She smiled with relief as Kate passed, the top of her writing pad visible above the pocket of her dress. Kate was the child anyone would wish for.

Sam was fiddling with spools of tape. He was experimenting with crowd noise.

'Sebastian.' Barbara touched her husband's arm anxiously. 'They should eat now. The whisky's nearly all gone!'

Interrupted, Sebastian turned back to his companion. 'According to Schwenk . . .'

'Seb,' persisted Barbara timidly.

'Oh, what?' asked Sebastian, his lips paler than his face with irritability.

'The buffet,' said Barbara. 'They must all be starving.'

'Ah,' cried Sebastian with sudden, unreal geniality. 'Eats. Is there enough?' he asked in a threatening aside to his wife.

'I think so,' she said imploringly. 'I bought so much.'

She purposely didn't add that she'd worked for two days getting it all ready, since that might sound like a reproach or a confession of weakness. If Seb wished to think that she did it all by magic then so he should. That version of things would reflect credit on them both – on him for being worthy of magic and on her for being capable of it.

The older, more practised guests had already eaten the pâté and the spinach quiche, and the rest were applying themselves to the turkey and ham and the rice and potato salads. Someone had stubbed out a cigar in a quarter of tomato. None of her mother's friends would do such a thing. These academic people were so absent-minded. She should be used to it by now, but she wasn't. The days of preparation and anxious thought – and then they all ate it up in the gaps between conversation, or left great heaps on their plates. Perhaps it was horrid – she couldn't tell, since she could neither eat nor taste after two days of cooking.

She pushed her way carefully through her guests.

A man on her right was complaining about publishers and the high price of books. 'They do it,' he said, *'pour encourager les auteurs.'*

Barbara sympathised deeply with people who were worried about the dreadful cost of living, but she had heard Sebastian remark, smiling nastily, that many of his colleagues should count themselves fortunate: they had such a splendid excuse when their books didn't sell.

At last she reached the bookcase in the other room, where she had hidden the after-dinner mints away from Sam. She was just in time to see her husband placing a piece of turkey with his fork in the damp red mouth of the wife of the Professor of Music, whose own hands were taken up with her glass and her embroidered ethnic evening bag, hung with tassels and studded with bits of mirror.

This playful, lascivious act was so uncharacteristic of Sebastian, and suited him so ill, that for a moment Barbara failed to recognise him. She felt suddenly deathly faint, and then she realised for herself what Sam had learnt at tea time and what everyone else had known for months.

Carefully she opened the bookcase and removed a book, *Platonis Opera*. She stared at it, wondering vaguely why it contained no chocolates.

Sebastian stepped away from his paramour and stood beside his wife. 'What is it, darling? What are you looking for?' he enquired with wholly unwonted solicitude.

'The sweets,' she answered him fearfully. Her husband was being kind to her in order to put himself in a good light with his lover.

Sebastian groped in the bookcase and handed her

25

the box. 'Here you are, darling,' he said, dismissing her.

Was Sebastian then, after all, stupid, she wondered. Did he not know that she knew, or didn't he care?

Sam was pleased to see the box in his mother's hands. He'd searched all the usual hiding places – she must have found somewhere different.

'No, Sam,' said Barbara, holding the box aside. 'You can have one later when everyone else has had one.'

She sounded funny, she looked funny. Sam temporarily lost his appetite for chocolate. Despite his own revolutionary tendencies he preferred his parents to behave sensibly. He pushed on with his tape recorder.

The rooms were inconveniently crowded and Sam was constantly halted by determined talkers engrossed in what they were saying and loth to move lest someone should seize the chance to interrupt with his own view of the topic under discussion. He found himself lodged behind a Regius Professor who was enquiring urbanely of a slender young man and a girl whether his desire to see the English keep their culture and heritage intact by mating only with persons of similar heritage made him a racist. As even Sam could see that the answer to this was yes, he couldn't understand why they stood there like a couple of lemons nodding and sipping.

Nearby the Canon was lecturing a small group on the subject of pride. 'We are told that pride is a vice,' he was saying, 'but is it not a virtue? I take pride in my country. I took pride in my school and my university. I take a humble pride in the fact that the chapter saw fit to elect me one of their number . . .'

He was nuts, decided Sam. The Canon was nuts, his father was nuts, they were all nuts. The biggest brains in Britain – and all nuts.

Sam and the university regarded each other with complete mutual incomprehension. It was inconceivable to Sam that anyone should wish to resemble or emulate his father or his father's colleagues, and inconceivable to *them* that anyone should not. He could see dimly that they were irrevocably separated by the age-old human problem – everyone's unshakable belief that everyone else either is, or wishes or deserves to be, like himself. Just as the healthy think the ill are malingering, so the ill think the healthy haven't yet recognised their own symptoms; as the homosexual think the heterosexual are lurking in the closet, so the heterosexual think the homosexual can be 'cured'; the old think the young desire their wisdom, the young that the old covet their youth, blacks that whites envy them their virility, whites that blacks wish to be white, the rich that the poor wish to be like them, the poor that the rich *are* like them, only richer and less happy. It all made for a great deal of needless fear and confusion, thought Sam with vague conviction.

Steering well clear of the Bursar, who had once, inadvisedly, cradled the back of Sam's head in his

27

hand, remarking that it was such a good shape, Sam sidled determinedly forward. He circled a don with a bemused expression listening to a long-haired girl describing the latest metropolitan party fun.

'They pass round a sheet of looking-glass,' the girl was explaining, 'and there are neat little rows of coke on it and each person takes a straw and sniffs up a row each.'

'Well, I think it's terrifying,' said an older woman. 'It *is* addictive, no matter what they say. It completely rots the membrane in the nose . . .'

'It's terribly expensive,' said the girl, rather wistfully.

'I always think it's such an *insipid* drink,' said the don, completely at sea.

Sam glanced at him through narrowed eyes, his expression of utter contempt giving him a brief resemblance to his father when faced with an undergraduate trying to derive a moral principle from a set of factual premises.

The Thrush, instantly distinguishable by her multicoloured, patched and banded peasant frock, was standing back-to-back with the Professor of Divinity, but Sam was wedged between him and an obviously troubled fat young person in spectacles who was addressing him.

'And they say that sodomy is one of the sins crying out to Heaven for vengeance . . .' the young man was saying.

'It all depends on what is meant by *sodomy*,' answered the divine stiffly, his narrow gold bracelet

28

– a gift from a friend – glinting shyly as he toyed with his glass.

Sam passed a group dominated by a frail old don speaking in exaggerated patrician accents by which he had not come honestly (all his relations had remained down their native pit). 'Mike . . .' he was saying to the group, 'Mike here is quite right to use the word "numinous". You see, Mike, when you say, Mike . . .' That meant Mike was a dumbo. All the old dons used the first names of dumbos a lot to put them at their ease.

'Silly ole fart,' muttered Sam. He exchanged a hostile glance with a lady whose elbow he had jogged, and pushed on.

He was next to the Thrush now. He lifted the microphone under his shirt to catch her words, half expecting her to declare her passion for his father. She was talking to another woman, similar to herself, but older.

'My mother got rather cross,' she was saying sweetly. 'She thought I was being unkind about Thalia.'

'There's really nothing unkind one *can* say about Thalia,' the other woman observed, laughing scornfully.

'No, of course,' agreed the Thrush, rather put out. Plainly she valued her connection with this Thalia, whoever she might be, and didn't care to have either Thalia, or her own familiarity with Thalia, undervalued. 'Superb musician,' she added decidedly. 'And did you know she has this *bird*?' The Thrush raised and lowered each plump shoulder in sudden animation as she thought of it.

'What kind of bird?' asked the older woman suspiciously. 'A real one?'

'A *real* one,' cried the Thrush ecstatically. 'This frightfully rare sort of parrot – it just flies loose all over the house.'

'My dear,' interrupted the other with quiet triumph. 'I have these friends in the country – the *most* lovely William-and-Maryish sort of house, one of the *most* beautiful houses in the country – and they have these macaws who fly *loose* around the valley. One's just riding along on one's pony and there's this sudden flash of blue. It's *most* lovely. They've picked all the window sills off, though,' she added in a sudden concession to banality.

The Thrush rallied. 'I wish you'd send them here then,' she said, in a brave attempt to keep the conversation going. She could hardly now return to Thalia's lone parrot, its house-bound brightness utterly dimmed by the brilliance of the outdoor macaws of her adversary's friends. 'There's the most ghastly concrete statue outside . . .'

'Oh no,' said the victorious one, putting the boot in. 'They wouldn't like that at all. They only like this lovely old stone!'

The Thrush smiled dejectedly. Sam almost felt sorry for her; but she was saying no more, so he pushed on until he came to the Professor of Music, who was making one of his jokes.

'He didn't so much cook the goose . . .'

' . . . as goose de cook,' chimed Sam, who had overheard a mathematician telling this one some weeks before. In this place mathematicians, scientists and musicians tended to make puns, often of a scatological kind. Teachers of English literature, on the other hand, though they tended to know nothing about anything except English literature – 'engliterates' his father called them – were sometimes a bit funnier – though on the whole they amused only themselves and one another. As for the few remaining classical scholars, most of their jokes were not merely old, but 2,000 years old, and expressed in dead languages. These jokes had plainly lost something in the course of time and were produced more as passwords than as attempts to communicate amusement, Sam thought. He called it showing off.

''s old,' he said, gazing accusingly up at the annoyed man, who couldn't be expected to know that Sam, in spite of his appearance and reputation, was, in matters of sex, an extremely proper, not to say prudish, child who had hoped to overhear him speak disapprovingly of the behaviour of the Thrush.

Brooding on the permissive society, Sam had reached the opposite wall, where his little sister had pinned someone's wife and was busy interrogating her on the works of Wordsworth.

'It's years since I went to school,' said the poor woman with a terrified laugh.

'I prefer the classical poets myself,' Kate informed her truculently. She was a big girl for her age, her

31

dress badly cut and the wrong length, the hem meeting the tops of her ankle socks. She was formidable.

'Gerra bed, cow,' said Sam.

'My brother isn't academic,' Kate told her victim with sibling satisfaction.

* * *

'A nice little piece of steak – braised, and some carrots,' said Mrs Marsh from the door of Mary's room. 'And Evelyn has brought you a lovely peach.'

'Lovely,' said Mary.

'Would you like Evelyn to come in and talk to you while you have your supper?' enquired Mrs Marsh, who often asked this question.

'No thank you,' said Mary, who often made this answer.

'Well, I think you're silly,' said her mother. 'Evelyn is very interesting once you get to know her.'

Evelyn, who lived across the Close, had taken up art in her mid-sixties. She had begun by painting by numbers but had now bought herself a cape and an easel and daily painted in freer style on the flasher-haunted downs. When she wasn't doing this she visited the lunatics who lived in vast numbers in an institution nearby. Many of them, she claimed, were 'as sane as you or I'. Some of them indeed consistently took her for one of themselves and would try to prevent her leaving for fear of the trouble and grief she would find in the world outside. This, Mary considered, showed some sense, for a recent fugitive had sought sanctuary in the church, where one of her mother's friends was arranging the flowers. 'I'm going to take my clothes off,' he had announced, perhaps as a further demonstration of his freedom, showing no sign of maniacal lust. 'If you do, I shall leave,' the flower-arranger had told him. But he did, so she fetched the vicar. 'Put on your vest,' the vicar demanded sternly. 'And your trousers and your shirt, and your socks and your shoes. And now go.' The denizens of Innstead were divided in their opinions of the vicar's action, some maintaining that he had shown strength of character and firmness of purpose, and some that he had behaved in an uncharitable and unchristian fashion. One old lady suggested that Jesus wouldn't have thrown the man out; but everyone, even the vicar's critics, thought this was going a little far. Society, after all, was quite different from what it had been in Jesus' day: the vicar should have alerted the social services, if not the police.

Mary found this sort of story interesting, but Evelyn preferred to talk of Caravaggio and chiaroscuro.

'She's got you a present,' said Mrs Marsh.

'Then I must get her one,' said Mary defiantly. Forgive us our Christmasses, she said to herself, as we forgive them who have Christmassed against us. It was an old joke of Mrs Marsh's, who would have been so pleased to hear it repeated aloud, but Mary kept silent. She had to be careful not to encourage her mother, not to raise false hopes.

'Is that the carrots burning?' asked Mrs Marsh, her hand cupped to her ear. She found her daughter difficult to talk to.

Later, when the percussion of pans and lids had stopped, Mary heard her mother talking to Evelyn. 'Such a good little hostess . . . The enormous parties . . .' she was saying of Barbara, and 'Anything . . . She could have done anything . . .' of Mary.

*   *   *

Barbara was trying to be brave. She was cold, and her hands shook. Her face was dry and wore a cut-out smile, as stiff and unnatural as a cardboard party mask, and she hardly knew what she was saying to the mobile faces around her as they opened and shut to speak or eat. She had told herself repeatedly that everyone else in this room had had extra-marital affairs and no one had died of it. No one minded any more – it was acceptable, it was smart, it was only human, it was 'sophisticated'. At the old-fashioned word she felt tears in her eyes. She had never even learned to be sophisticated and now that everything had passed beyond the very concept she was lost – a stranger among her friends. 'Oh the smoke,' she said, to explain her overflowing eyes.

'I'm sorry,' said some woman offendedly, flapping at the air in front of her mouth to clear it.

'No,' said Barbara. 'Oh no . . .' Oh, she thought, I wasn't brought up like that. I was brought up to be faithful and polite. I don't smoke or complain when other people do. What's happening to me? I didn't mean it, I didn't mean it.

It was a good party. Everyone except herself seemed to be having a lovely time. Apart from the autochthonous notables there was a sprinkling of peers and politicians, and someone had briefly brought the currently fashionable Russian dissident. He had a spoilt, invalidish air – partly because he was so well wrapped up in scarf, gloves and hat and partly because of the unnatural deference accorded him.

Barbara herself unconsciously shared the feeling of intermittent unease that afflicted most of the university population who, while confident that their institution was the centre of the universe, were also vaguely aware of a certain provincialism. Those dons who could afford it had flats or even houses in London and at least a few friends not directly connected with the academic world.

One of these desirable outsiders was speaking to her now, asking after her sister. Why, she wondered irritably, did she think of him first as Mary's friend rather than as Seb's editor? Her sister had a way of defining people by her relationship with them, and while Barbara loved Mary this was no time to be reminded of ancient jealousies.

'She's all right, Hunter,' she snapped, realising from his tone that he already knew perfectly well how Mary was. Mary, she thought distractedly, remembering with panic that she had liked the Thrush, had liked having musical friends. Having no particular gifts of any kind herself, she had determined to appreciate music more than anyone else. She had pointed out as often as possible, to whoever would listen, how much she appreciated music. And now even that was ruined. Her friend, her interest and her husband – all lost to a mouthful of turkey.

'Are *you* all right, Barbara?' asked Hunter.

'I think so,' she said pitifully. 'I might sit down.'

Hunter ousted an elderly gentleman from the nearest chair and placed his hostess in it.

She was ashamed, she was frightened. But she was going to cry – here. And now.

Sam switched on his tape.

Greatly amplified, the voice of the Canon was heard: '. . . a humble pride in the fact that the chapter . . .' For a moment the Canon thought he'd gone mad. He stared round wildly.

'. . . the *most* lovely William-and-Maryish sort of house,' roared the amplifier.

'. . . goose de cook,' it informed them at an unbearable pitch of sound.

Sebastian seized the plug and pulled it out. There was total silence save for his wife's now reasonably restrained sobbing.

'See how you have upset your mother,' said Sebastian quietly to his son. 'I hope you are satisfied.'

Of course after that there was laughter: nervous, and in a few cases artificial, laughter – but laughter none the less. People bent down to peer kindly at Barbara's damp and twitching face. They lightly squeezed her forearm, or patted her shoulder with quick consoling movements, not wishing to imply that there was anything seriously wrong but eager to express sympathy. A few of the harder, coarser guests regarded her sideways, with disgust.

Hunter, gazing into the distance, put his arm about her and turned her head against his hip. He stroked her ear once, patted her hair and then hurried away – but not soon enough. There stirred in Barbara that unreasoning affinity of the newly hatched gosling for the nearest solid object. Crawling painfully from her shell of rejection, she permitted herself the beginnings of a fixation on Hunter – as doomed to disappointment as the infant goose seeking succour of a fox-terrier or a cardboard box.

She raised her head and smiled – which made her look a little mad.

'Her sister is very ill,' Sebastian told his guests discreetly. 'Barbara is under great strain.'

Reassured, they resumed their enjoyment of the party.

Hunter sought out Sebastian's American publisher, of whom he was in charge. He didn't really think that Otis Mauss would have been particularly offended or disturbed by the recent events, but his unusual sense of responsibility drove him to make certain. Mr Mauss, as he had expected, was standing happily alone, gazing about and holding his glass with both hands. He was an undemanding and amiable man who, Hunter felt, thought of the English with whom he had to deal as a bunch of clever monkeys who were not to be judged by normal American standards. Hunter himself thought of Otis

Mauss as rather more foreign and strange than a dynastic Chinaman.

'Have you talked to some nice people?' he asked.

'Yessure,' said Mr Mauss.

Hunter wondered which they had been and looked around for an untried likely victim. Most of the people present had good manners, so he reached out and seized an elbow at random.

Barbara was sickened to see the Thrush talking to Sebastian's editor. It was plain to her that the immoral woman meant to infiltrate every aspect of Seb's life. Barbara felt as though she were drowning, falling through a bottomless space of lovelessness with no hand to catch or prevent her.

Hunter was pleased to be able to introduce his charge to the Thrush. Although in the wider world she wouldn't have passed muster in the qualifying round for Miss Llandudno, by university standards she was considered exceptionally beautiful. His conscience clear, he chatted happily to the Canon.

*　　*　　*

The wind had dropped. The lamp lit a corner of the window pane, illuminating a swarm of snowflakes, and the smokeless fuel in the fireplace burned brightly. Mary, her book open and unread on her lap, listened to her mother and Evelyn talking in the kitchen. They always sat there in the evenings after W.I. meetings, perched on high blue stools, drinking coffee out of mugs and eating biscuits from a blue tin.

'You must first make a little list,' said Evelyn. 'Two little lists. One for Christmas Day itself and one for the other days.'

Mary could sense her mother's irritation.

'I've *done* that,' said Mrs Marsh. 'I could *paper* the kitchen with little lists. I'm trying to think where to put everybody.'

'Well, *you're* staying with me,' said Evelyn. 'I thought you'd decided . . .'

'I mean for lunch on Christmas Day,' said Mrs Marsh. 'Mary's in the dining room. The kitchen's too small, and as I've got rid of the dining table I shall have to put up two small tables in the sitting room, and if the worst comes to the worst the children can eat on the stairs. There's you and me, and Barbara and Mary, and Kate and Sam and Sebastian and Mary's Hunter. There are three straight chairs, these two stools, the pouffe, and two people will have to sit in armchairs with cushions, but it makes the tables so crowded.'

'Then put the children in the hall,' suggested Evelyn helpfully.

'I'm *going* to do that if I have to,' said Mrs Marsh, sounding, as she spoke, as if she were grinding her teeth.

'You were silly to sell all your dining-room things,' said Evelyn, and Mary held her breath. But her mother answered mildly enough and absently, as though she were already thinking of something else.

'Mary could hardly have slept on the table or in the sideboard,' she said. 'I think I'll put Barbara and Kate in one room, and Sebastian and Sam in the other. The children are really too old to sleep together.'

Someone ran the tap and turned on the electric kettle and the voices became inaudible. Mary twisted herself round to look at the small vertiginous area of falling snow and heard no more.

*　　　*　　　*

It was growing late, and Hunter's eyes were a little blurred.

'I must get you back to the Savoy,' he said to Mr Mauss.

'That's very good of you,' said Mr Mauss equably, putting down his glass and looking round for the door.

'Well, in a minute,' said Hunter. 'I must say goodbye.'

'Oh, me too,' said Mr Mauss, quite unruffled.

Hunter kissed Barbara's cheek – something he hadn't done before. 'It was a lovely party,' he said. 'I'm so looking forward to Christmas Day.'

Barbara gazed at him silently, waiting for some explanation of this odd remark.

'I'm going to Mary's for lunch,' he explained. 'Your mother asked me.'

Barbara smiled slowly. Somewhere in that area of the human mind where the wish is father to the thought activity was taking place. Hunter, Barbara decided, had wangled this invitation in order to be with her. Not even his description of her mother's house as Mary's annoyed her now. Hunter desired her, and Sebastian should be taught a lesson.

She didn't move or speak, merely smiled a slightly batty smile and watched him walk away.

The smile alarmed Hunter. Being in the world of books he was familiar with lunacy in all its forms and that smile reminded him of something. He had last seen it, he remembered, on the face of an author who had written a book combining the basic principles of zoology with psycho-analysis which he believed beyond all doubt would change the course of the world. He shuddered. Sebastian was a tiresome fellow, he thought censoriously, and being lazy-minded about human relations he didn't bother to ask himself why Sebastian's infidelity should bring that particular look of loony expectation to Barbara's face. Seizing Mr Mauss, he made for the door.

Kate, flushed with praise and approval and quite above herself, rebuked her brother for making their mummy cry.

Sam had remained at the party, prominently placed in the centre of the room, in order to save face. He hadn't enjoyed it, and this was too much.

'Fuck off,' he said very loudly.

Hunter had to intervene. Seeing Sebastian's expression, he dropped Mr Mauss and stepped in front of Sam, wondering as he did so why it was that so many publishers were regarded by their authors as mother, father, guide, philosopher and friend (not to mention pimp, psychiatrist, midwife, bank) and, what's more, so often felt it incumbent upon themselves to fulfil these expectations. He himself didn't like authors much, especially Seb Lamb.

'My dear,' he said, seizing Sebastian by the upper arm. 'Otis wishes to say goodbye to you.'

'G'bye,' said Mr Mauss docilely. 'Seeya m'next trip. Come to Dallas.'

Stepping thankfully through the front door into the cold air of the stone town, Hunter was yet again pounced on by a Lamb.

'Sam's gone,' Kate gabbled excitedly. 'He's run away, and Mummy's gone after him, without her coat.'

Handing Mr Mauss back into the hallway, Hunter took off down the street. Barbara was wringing her hands on the next corner and peering despairingly to right and left. Twice before Sam had been brought home by the police and she was sick of it. She couldn't bear any more . . .

Hunter saw Sam first, across the road, standing in a bus queue with one or two old people who were talking to each other because it was so cold.

'Sam,' called Barbara. 'Come here at once.'

Sam stared deafly ahead.

'Sam,' repeated Barbara on the edge of hysteria.

'A'right, O.K.,' said Sam, loping nonchalantly across the road.

The old people gazed, silenced, at their departing companion wondering perhaps whether this was an abduction, but not very interested.

*   *   *

Mary awoke early to a sky the colour of writing paper, very high and blandly indifferent. She wished she could throw something human, something bad, at that pale and careless sky – beyond which, she suspected, the little gods were playing selfish games.

The snow had gone in the night, there was no wind and the day was as still as that day in Aulis for which Iphigenia paid the price.

'Nice cup of hot tea?' yelled her mother from the kitchen, going on to complain in normal tones that the snow had melted and she did think for once they might have had a white Christmas.

'I feel like a great white vegetable,' said Mary, unanswerably.

'*What?*' cried her mother, dashing from one door to the next and viewing her daughter with angry alarm. She was a gardener herself and had no love for those horrid, neglected, water-retentive tubers, blanched beyond recovery. 'Your breakfast's ready,' she said, panting a little.

No one could leave without breakfast. If, regularly, nice little meals were brought for her straying daughter, Mary wouldn't be able to leave. When would she find the time if tea was ready, or her milk drink with the skin skimmed off? Mary wasn't really ill-mannered. Mrs Marsh planned ever-widening palisades of breakfast, elevenses, lunch, tea, dinner, supper, to contain her child.

Mary was quite sorry for her. It seemed hard that mothers should be the means of letting into the trap that was life those creatures they loved best in the world. For despite their designation the entrance was not entrancing, nor the exit exciting. And the space between held more of bitterness than was promised with the salt, the balm, the joyous clear water and the white cloth of baptism.

* * *

Mrs Marsh got out her fur-lined boots. They were slightly too small – she was vain about her little feet and refused to admit that they had spread since her dancing days.

She went into Mary's room to pull her boots on and discuss what she should buy at the shops. The discussion was largely conducted with herself, since Mary, unlike Barbara, wasn't interested in shopping.

'Old Soames had some nice *geese*,' said Mrs Marsh grimacing, pulling at the back of her boot and stamping down on the final word. 'Except a goose would be no good for all of us – just bone and buckets of grease. Daddy used to like a nice goose though, with a sharp apple sauce. I mustn't forget to pick up my jacket from the cleaners. Is there anything you want?'

'No,' said Mary. 'Thanks.'

'I'll get you some eggs,' said Mrs Marsh. 'They'll be fresh today. You ought to come with me,' she added. 'You could do with some new make-up, and it's no good me buying it when you're not there.' She looked resentfully at Mary's pale face. 'You look like a toad's tummy,' she said to it, not really addressing her daughter as a whole. She believed that women felt better with a touch of make-up on – no matter how old or sad or beaten the face. Her daughter was cold and alien as a puddock, a bright hard jewel of rage burning in her head.

Mary thought it would be diverting to paint her nose with lipstick and her teeth with eyeshadow and annoy her mother. 'There's no point,' she said, which annoyed her mother more.

'There's *always* point,' said Mrs Marsh. 'Look your best and you feel your best.'

'You should go if you're going,' said Mary. 'It'll snow.'

Alone in the house, she stood up. She could go into the kitchen if she liked, or the other room, or even upstairs. She could scream if she liked, though not too loudly or they'd hear her next door.

At Melys y Bwyd a flock of white geese grazed by a stream where the lane passed through a farmyard, overhung and dark with trees. She could see them – so perfectly shaped and delineated that they were like excisions from some more clearly conceived reality, making even the barn cats seem amateurly constructed and the scuttling and fussing hens bungled – mere mistakes.

Then there was Robin stencilled against her awareness like the geese against the Advent darkness, clear and preternaturally real, quite unlike her tweaked and harassed relations, and shining always with a radiance that graced the living only when they stood against the snow.

'Well,' she said aloud. She was back in the lane going to the graveyard. It was winter – winter, so there would be berries in the rusted hedgerows, blood-hued from bright scarlet to arterial purple, the fruit of the wild rose and the hawthorn and elder and holly scattered against the cold sky, as though some wounded god, running, had shaken a bleeding hand in irritable pain. The streams that ran alongside the hedgerows would be frozen to steel and the dead grass stiff with frost. She could feel the wind encircling her head and tears chill on her face.

In the summer there had been no tears. There had been no whipping wind, no onions, no small pains to bring them, and she couldn't weep for Robin – weeping was insufficient and inappropriate. The birds of the air should mourn for Robin and all the vast hordes of the dead.

The sun had shone with great heat for Robin's last day above the earth. It had been a shadowless day, without measure, so that the flies that rose from the dung heaps in the lane had seemed no less beautiful than the wild flowers strewn under and over the hedgerows. Shy gravediggers, half conceal-ing their rude spades, stood in the rib-high grasses at the unkempt edge of the graveyard, nodding apologetically if they caught anyone's eye.

They had dared to lower Robin in a box into a pit in that dry graveyard, filled with sun.

It hadn't been then, nor did it seem now, an occasion for tears.

* * *

Mrs Marsh plodded towards the shops, her fur hat pulled well down over her ears, dragging her wheeled basket behind her. She enjoyed Christmas, with the darkness and the light in the shops. The sky away over the city was yellow through grey, like old rubbed Sheffield plate, but the High Street was bright with oranges and lemons.

She waited in an ill-defined queue at the green-grocer's, secretly enjoying the smells of celery and damp paper and apples. All the ladies present knew each other slightly and spoke. 'Hello,' they said, and 'Isn't it cold?' Most were well and casually dressed, their hair tipped and streaked with blonde.

'Hullo, Mrs Marsh,' said someone running in from the street.

'Hullo, Vera,' said Mrs Marsh. This was her next-door neighbour, whose hair was grey-brown and untended, though partially obscured by a felt hat. She had very small eyes.

'I'm run off my feet,' said Vera. 'I know it's only Dennis and I, but I never seem to stop. How's Mary?' She lowered her voice for this question, and her little eyes crossed as she looked into Mrs Marsh's face.

'She's fine,' said Mrs Marsh. 'It'll take time . . .'

'Of course,' agreed Vera.

'. . . but she'll be fine,' concluded Mrs Marsh. She didn't want to discuss her daughter with this dumpy little creature. She had overheard Evelyn explaining

47

Mary's illness to Vera. 'Complete physical collapse,' Evelyn had said in knowledgeable tones. 'One day her legs just gave way and down she went. Psychological, of course . . .' Mrs Marsh had interrupted with a quite unnecessary reminder to Evelyn that she was expected for Christmas lunch. Then she had gone on, even more unnecessarily, to invite Vera to come for drinks in the evening. She couldn't understand why she'd done it: she was neighbourly and hospitable by disposition but she didn't crave the company of Vera and Dennis.

'Don't forget you're coming for a drink on Christmas Day,' she said.

'Oh, we won't,' said Vera confidently. 'We're looking forward to it.'

Mrs Marsh hauled her basket along to the dry cleaners and collected her velvet jacket. She didn't really need very much shopping. She was out for the pleasure of it, to see people she knew and to look in the shop windows, and to be away from the house for a while – on the run. She bought a dozen eggs and wondered if she had deserved a cup of coffee. No, she decided, she hadn't. She walked back to the greengrocer's to buy some grapes for Mary and some nuts for the birds.

*   *   *

Barbara was frenziedly packing. She had turned off the central heating, or hoped she had. She could never quite work the various controls, and Seb, who

could, she was certain, if he wanted to, grew so
irritable when she asked him to do it. She had
emptied the fridge and given all the left-over food
from the party to her cleaning lady, who in turn
would give what was suitable to the cat and throw
the rest away. Barbara knew she would do this but
didn't care as long as the shame of wastefulness
couldn't be attributed directly to her. She and the
cleaning lady had scraped squashed olives and dog-
ends off the stained mushroom-coloured carpet, done
what they could for a cigarette burn on the walnut
table and rather feebly shaken the brown-and-white
patterned curtains to release the smoke. The house
had grown shabbier and shabbier through Sam's
short life and a series of parties.

Now she went alone through the bedrooms. Shirts,
underpants, socks, ties, shaving things for Seb. As
she packed, she inspected all his garments for signs
of infidelity – lipstick, strange hairs, semen – but
found nothing. No notes in the pockets of his suits,
no jewelled clips caught in his vests. Seb was so neat
and clever, she reflected with a prideful hatred.

She found Sam's leather trousers and his worn,
smelly, thick-soled suede shoes, which she had agreed
to bring on the understanding that he wouldn't wear
them. When Sam had asked 'Whassa point o'
bringin' 'em den?', she had burst into tears, and
Sam had retired in the sullen, despairing rage of the
adolescent.

In Kate's room she carefully chose the best clothes
from her chest of drawers and the little wardrobe

covered with pictures of baby deer and rabbits. She packed Kate's notebooks and drawings to show Grandma, and sat teddy on her bed to await her return.

Then she packed the few things she herself would need – her crimson frock for Christmas Day, two petticoats, two best pairs of knickers, two uplift bras, all her tights, her tartan skirt and her purple jumper. She would wear her tweed skirt and the green jumper and be prepared for any occasion. She put in her nightie of cream viyella, a packet of sanitary towels and the things for her face. She mustn't forget her deodorant and her bottle of lavender water. Finally, the Christmas presents: a box of handmade chocs for her mother and a jar of real caviar for Mary. She was unconscious that the reason why she had chosen these comestibles was that her native thrift rebelled against giving anything more durable to the aged or to one who might be terminally ill. Her husband's and children's presents were already in the boot of the car, and she wondered without much hope whether they would like them.

She went once more round the house to make sure she had left nothing that would smoulder or moulder – no cigarette ends in the waste-paper baskets, or Sam's crusts under cushions. There was a fresh burn on the stair carpet she hadn't noticed before.

Taking a tranquillizing pill she locked the door, pulling it several times to make sure, and walked round to pick up the car.

Sam was sitting in the back with his feet dangling over the front seat.

'I thought you were with Kate at Emily's house,' said Barbara. 'I was just coming to get you.'

'Wuz boring,' said Sam.

'And how did you get into the car?' demanded his mother.

'Wuz open,' said Sam.

Barbara knew perfectly well that it couldn't have been, and was shaken again by the awful fear that her son was a natural criminal.

They picked up Kate, who was waiting in her red coat, from Emily's house. Then they collected Seb from his college, where he was polishing a paper. He detested being taken away from his work and muttered as he followed them to the car.

Sebastian had devoted his life and his career to the proposition that words should be used with tremendous care, that no statement should be made that wasn't capable of precise utterance, and that anyone who couldn't say exactly what he meant should keep his trap shut. In the heady days earlier in the century when this novel idea first began to gather adherents, it was held by them that a massive, invincible engine was being constructed that would overturn all false, all mistaken structures of human thought – such as religious belief – and clear the ground for true human progress. But as time passed it began to seem that this tool resembled not so much a mighty bulldozer as that useful but scarcely earth-shaking, and indeed slightly anachronistic, implement – the thing for taking stones out of horses' hooves. Sebastian didn't care. His philosophy perfectly fitted his personality, and he had nearly finished his latest book – *would* have finished it, if it hadn't been for Christmas.

'Would you go in the back, Seb?' asked his wife.

'*I'm* not going in the back,' said Seb, getting in the front.

'Then you children mustn't quarrel,' said Barbara. 'It's dangerous when I'm driving.' Her mother used to say to her and Mary: 'Birds in their little nests agree.' Mary at a young age had denied it, pointing out that birds in their little nests spent most of their time trying to shove the other birds over the edge. Mary had always been cynical – and ungrateful – thought Barbara, hot with anxiety and resentment that so many of her relations should be so unsatisfactory.

Sam suddenly felt furiously sorry for his mother. In her sheepskin jacket and her sheepskin mittens she looked like an inverted bell-wether. (All the university wives wore sheepskin when they drove or shopped because they thought it unassuming and practical and ladylike; but, if they had only realised, it was actually merely sheeplike.) Also, her dark curly hair was in a mess and the end of her nose was red. He kicked Kate, who immediately howled.

'Oh,' cried Barbara, on a breaking note, earning herself a look of disgust from Sebastian, who turned to address his children . . .

*   *   *

Mrs Marsh beat around the house like a moth. Her movements, though disciplined and deliberate, were to Mary as irritating and alarming as the pointless vacillations of a large insect. She was flapping dusters over spotless surfaces, counterpanes over immaculate beds, embroidered guest-towels over the bathroom rails, thin little rugs on the gleaming slippery parquet of the hall. There was so much useless cloth in this house.

Mary thought nostalgically of winding sheets, of linen ripped for bandages, of sails – of taking to the sea uncluttered and cold as a rafter of bones. House-work should be done in secret or not at all. A busy woman was a reproach, insistent and disturbing, a reprimand to the silent scholar or the idle dead, announcing, with each flourish that life was to be lived, that there was no room in the habitations of the living for the grey peace of dust and decay, that the virtuous must polish and wash and sweep and scrub – scouring and mopping, relentless as time.

Mary just sat by the window. Pain and rage and guilt lay in her mind as still as fish in a stagnant pool. In the dull depths she could also discern the untidy lineaments of shame. During the painstaking unravelling of feeling into thought, she had realised that she would have preferred Robin to live on, suffering, rather than herself suffer the anguish of loss. There's love, she said, astonished. What a peculiar thing! Yet she neither wished nor had the

53

time to dislike herself. It was hardly worth the trouble. She had never bothered to rejoice when she had been 'lucky Mary' – so lucky that passing people asked (or so it seemed) 'Who is that lucky one? Is it some princess?' and she would answer, not triumphantly, 'No, it is lucky Mary. She has found her heart's desire and this is her happy-ever-after.' She was unsuited to life. Perhaps, despite the evidence of her mother's devotion, she hadn't come through the usual channel, but had dropped from a branch, treating as she did even happiness as a caged ape a banana, suspiciously and all thumbs.

'They'll be here soon,' said her mother joyfully from the doorway, flapping a silk hankie up the sleeve of the smart little frock she had just put on. It would do Mary so much good to have the family here to take her out of herself. It was so good of Barbara to be coming here instead of going to Seb's parents even though it was their turn: she hoped they would mind, since she knew they thought Barbara wasn't really worthy of their son, living as they did in the country, keeping dogs and getting mud on their boots. That life wouldn't have suited Mrs Marsh at all, but this didn't prevent her from realising that they considered her socially inferior.

Sebastian's father, the judge, was a complacent man with a high colour, the set mouth of one who has never been contradicted and a voice which sounded as though he was perpetually swallowing a mouthful of expensive whisky together with a few fox hairs. Sebastian's mother, the bishop's daughter, resembled her husband, except that her voice was high – like a curlew's cry. Neither of them in their whole lives, as far as anyone knew, had ever suffered any reversal of fortune. Even the state of the nation, which they attributed to the greed and sloth of the working classes and to something they called the 'politics of envy', didn't particularly dismay them, and they were waiting with a certain retributory anticipation for the tide to turn. Mrs Marsh felt towards them the slight fear and hostility, mixed awkwardly with wondering respect, that each layer of the English class structure feels for the layer just above it. They were both, of course – Mrs Marsh and the in-laws – united in their admiration of the monarchy, since the royal succession was secure and no jumped-up entrepreneur or foreigner could aspire to it. The absence of possibility had a soothing effect on the caste system.

Sebastian's sister, Jennifer, had married a large rich man who still played rugby and got even muddier than the rest of the family. Mary said they'd met in Harrods and bought each other there, but Mrs Marsh thought highly of Harrods and wasn't consoled.

'I'll sit in the Close and wait for Barbara,' said Mary, adding to her mother's pleasure.

Her motive was selfish. She wished to save herself pain, to be warned of the arrival, since if she were to relax and drift the shortest distance into her reveries of wilderness the shock of recall would be unpleasant. Even now she hated to hear a knock

55

at the door. At Melys y Bwyd the doors had never been locked. The old Welsh tradition still held in that remote valley. Friends of the house walked straight in, calling 'Is anybody home?' A knock at the door meant that strangers had come among them.

The two young men had knocked for a long time before she heard them – as the bird had knocked at the window of Melys y Bwyd in another dawn, unthinking harbinger of despair in the damp soft greyness as the moonless night ebbed. She had tapped back at the bird through the brittle membrane of glass, waved her arms at it mockingly, shouted at it. Sad, black, desperate thing – it wouldn't go away. That means a death, the Welsh had told her. The policemen, too, had come to tell her of a death. She seemed to remember that she'd thanked them and they'd offered to make her a cup of tea . . . Doors had lost significance, since not one would ever open to admit Robin. Walls and windows too now possessed a strange ambivalence. Dangerous and circumscribing, they no longer represented safety or comfort but merely translated the wilderness into a view – into a humanised, rationalised vision of infinity, the measure of which it was impossible to formulate. Later that evil morning, leaving the house, because arrangements had to be made, she had smelled the flowering privet fresh and shining from the night's rain, glimpsed the racing liberated sky and been appalled by a moment of glittering joy, as intense as any she had ever known. She wondered sometimes whether she had gone mad then and stayed mad ever since, since in order to tolerate the intolerable it was necessary to change the rules, or at least one's conception of them. She had heard the cuckoo that spring too, while she was walking down the lane. 'Jesu Grist,' the roadman had said, busy giving the hedgerow a short-back-and-sides. 'There's bad luck.' It seemed it was only safe to hear the cuckoo call while you stood on greenery – leaves or grass, even a sprig of parsley. To hear it while you walked on barren ground was a poor omen. Mary wished he'd told her earlier. She would never have left the garden, would have made her shoes of salad stuff.

'Sit on the bench,' said Mrs Marsh. 'You'll be nice and sheltered there.'

The bench circled the cedar that grew in the middle of the little lawn. To the cedar's unprotesting trunk was nailed a shingle – cut obliquely to retain the greatest amount of bark – deeply incised with the gilded words 'Honeyman's Close'. It interrupted the flow of the squirrel as he poured up and down collecting the delicacies that were put out for him by the residents. Sometimes he sat on it, and his benefactors took photographs of him to send to their relations in New Zealand. Round the lawn stood a dozen new little houses in what had been the garden of a larger house. The high surrounding wall remained, but the garden was cut up into gravel paths wide enough for cars and the cedar was all that was left of the original trees. New trees and shrubs had been planted – all evergreen, because they were better value for money, retaining their decorative properties the year round and not dropping their messy leaves all over the place like the spendthrift deciduous varieties.

Mary was quite alone. Most of the neighbours were childless. Some had grown-up children who had long since left home, and those who had young children had been careful to have so few that they could afford to send them to boarding school and take them away on holidays. No tricycles lay about, no balls, no discarded garments. Good, thought Mary. There were only the birds, summer-fat in midwinter in this bird-loving environment. There were no cats; and dogs were discouraged, except for old Miss Jones's scottie, who was permitted, because his mistress was said to be of county descent and therefore at once deserved him and could be relied upon to look after him. The people at No. 5 who owned a chain of hairdressing shops had originally moved in with a bedlington, a boxer and a dachshund looking like an incomplete set of old-fashioned pictorial cigarette cards, but although there had been no unpleasantness they had soon realised that dogs didn't fit in to the Close and had given them away to friends who lived in ampler surroundings. There had been angry consternation when the Close heard that a policeman was to move in to the house next door to Mrs Marsh's. The neighbours were relieved to learn that he was a Chief Inspector, but still they wished he'd chosen a different place of retirement. 'He'll bring his alsatian or his dobermann pinscher,' prophesied the lady from No. 5. They were all quite surprised when he didn't.

The squirrel was accepted – nay, loved – since he was a solitary celibate squirrel and caused no trouble at all, living as he did up a tree, an honorary bird. Had he been one of a group, things would have been different and the council called in. As there were no children there were no pet rabbits. Moles, voles and mice were severely discouraged, and any resident of the Close would have died if he had met a rat. Foxes were said to forage occasionally in the dustbins of people who lived nearer to the downs, but they hadn't yet ventured in to the Close. There were no toads, frogs or newts, since the garden pond had been filled in. And as for bears – fierce, unfriendly, foul-breathed and not very bright (when transfixed by the spear of the plucky Finn, they would grasp the shaft in their long-clawed paws and, rather than attempt to wrench it out, push it further into their black ursine heart) – it was inconceivable that a bear should venture within a thousand miles of Innstead. Yet in every house in the Close there were effigies, icons and books of tales about all these animals; china statues of moles and toads in bonnets and shawls; watercolours of mice up cornstalks and rabbits and frogs in rings with fairies. Each resident had kept his own or his children's teddy bear and the children's classics which had sustained their youth. One year the toy manufacturers had intro-duced a new line of teddies bearing the facial simili-tude of the Poet Laureate (himself a teddy-bear

59

fancier), and a number of children had been badly frightened.

The totem of the English was a small animal — furry, stuffed and articulate. Winnie the Pooh vied with the Queen (God trailing in the distance) for the forefront of the mind of the English middle class. An English diplomat imprisoned in a foreign country, kept for month upon month in solitary confinement, thrown into spiritual confrontation with himself, emerged from captivity and wrote a book about a baby seal who preferred T-bone steak to fish. Even the leaders of the political parties had come to resemble little animals. On the left an old teddy; his stuffing, his credibility, leaking a little now. On the right a mouse — a shop mouse, her head stuck in a yellowed meringue, a mean little mouse bred on cheese rind and broken biscuit and the nutritionless, platitudinous parings of a grocer's mind. The erstwhile leader of the middle party was a fox — rather tired now — his fine brush matted and drooping, his cunning mask despondent. Did any other people, Mary wondered, apart from Red Indians, make such a fuss of creatures which in reality they were in the habit of chasing, shooting, poisoning, trapping or beating to death with sticks? Mrs Marsh had bought Kate a book about rabbits, 'suitable for the older child' but widely read by supposedly normal adults.

Barbara's car must be quite near now. It would probably be inching down the crowded derelict road that led out of the metropolis, past boarded shop windows, car-hire firms, Chinese take-aways, shops

selling saris, pram and bicycle shops, stretches of
Georgian houses ruined and blackened by despair,
municipal offices neat and well-lit, small factories,
the Baths, very low churches (theologically speaking) with very large notices of warning and exhorta-
tion aimed principally at the godfearing immigrant
community. Then it would follow a stretch of road
lined with huge pubs, small houses and car dumps.
This was a route that missed the best of Innstead –
the private schools, discreet hospitals, well-tended
gardens and the old village street, so carefully
restored and maintained. It merely cut across a small
section of the downs and came out again into a
wilderness of intersecting highways mad with cars
speeding through the dead common, asphyxiated
bushes and bleached grass that shrank away from
the roadside. Stained paper drifted about these
bushes. Under them lay old petrol cans and –
mysteriously – the rusting discarded organs of motor
cars. This was dangerous country, where no one
walked save for the occasional amateur botanist in
search of the elusive winter aconite, or young couples
driven from the comfort of the three-piece-suite by
men and boys intent on Match of the Day. The
walkers would be as likely to stumble upon the
tights-strangled bodies of young women thrust into
plastic bags and bound with electrical flex as find
the aconite or peace with each other. It was always
bad ground, ill-used and perilous, that lay between
town and country. Even the piglets that sometimes
escaped from the few decaying farms eschewed it

and ran squealing down the road that led to the coast. It was astonishing, unbelievable, that a short though nervous and hurried walk across the intersections and through the five sets of traffic lights would bring the pedestrian in a minute to the saccharine silence of Honeyman's Close, to the unique, inimitable cleanliness and warmth of the small, prosperous suburban home, to the well-appointed, walled, enfoliaged, grass-laid peace of modest but sufficient wealth – neater, more stable and more contained than great riches, and far more comfortable, but not like the wild sweetness of Melys y Bwyd, 'Sweet is Life' . . .

The sudden loud rebuke of a motor horn gave Mary warning. Whenever Sebastian was in the car something happened to Barbara's driving that caused other motorists to sound their horns, swear or take evasive action according to temperament.

With a splash of gravel Barbara drew up.

They looked oddly at home, thought Mary – not at all out of place, as her own few friends always did. This cloistral suburb had more in common with the university than she had realised. Intellect was lacking here certainly, but exclusivity and the calm conviction of rightness were not. Honeyman's Close too had its own aims, values and customs set apart from the rest of the world. Therefore it ill became Sebastian Lamb to gaze about him with such weariness. Only Sam was incongruous, and Mary found it no easier than anyone else to imagine a situation in which he might not be.

The worst was over now. Her relations had leapt into the silence with noisy cries of greeting, like people on first reaching the sea, but now were merely moving about in it, talking in normal tones.

Two opposite doors stood open in the Close, Evelyn framed in one and Mrs Marsh running from the other.

'You've arrived,' announced Evelyn welcomingly.

Sebastian was forced to respond in agreement since Barbara, Kate and Mrs Marsh were all mixed up together and Sam seldom responded to anything. Sebastian raised and lowered his hand, his tweed hat still on his head. Hat-raising had gone out, but Evelyn hadn't been told so and thought him very rude for an educated man.

'I'll see you all later,' she said in the voice she used on the telephone, and closed her door.

*   *   *

Barbara stood with her mother and daughter in the middle of the little bedroom hoping she wasn't going to cry again. It was so warm and soft and gently lit, and her mother was so pleased to see her. Barbara was just beginning to recover from her lifelong and entirely mistaken conviction that Mary was their mother's favourite, only to be presented by Sebastian with a new, even more dangerous, rival. It wasn't fair.

Mrs Marsh fussed, full of joy, about the double bed upon which, obscuring the pale-green counterpane, lay an assortment of things which she was going to give to her younger child. 'Aunt Gwennie's fur,' she said, 'and some beautiful underwear she never wore. And the cashmere sweater she bought in the summer sales – I know because I went with her to get it – and her dear little watch, and her jade brooch . . .'

She stopped, aware of a lack of enthusiasm. Kate had seized the watch and was crying, 'Oh Mummy, look. Oh Granny, what a dear little watch. I always wanted a little watch . . .'

Mrs Marsh looked slowly at Barbara with the beginnings of apprehension. Another sad daughter would be too much to bear. Mary had been quite indifferent to all the pretty things. 'It looks as though there'd been a cat burglary,' she'd said, 'rather than a death. All those little thievables.' Mrs Marsh had wondered then what Mary had done with Robin's belongings – but there hadn't been many . . . She had begun to understand, with real fear, that Mary was *waiting* – such terrible, greedy waiting as she had never contemplated. The woman who had been her pretty, merry little daughter was waiting for the dead to return and, failing that, was waiting, as a lover waits, for death to come and get her.

Mrs Marsh could think of no suitable rebuke to fit such a case. 'The coat is a bit big on me,' she said uncertainly to Barbara, 'but you'd look lovely in it.'

Lovely. Suddenly Barbara's misery fell away. She would look lovely on Christmas Day. Hunter was coming. They would walk together up the hill to the old village and she would drink something sweet in the nice pub with the open fire and the genial landlord. Seb would come to find her and see her laughing at Hunter's conversation and Hunter sitting a little too close. Then she would choose between them . . .

She put on the coat and straightened her shoulders.

'You look lovely, Mummy,' piped Kate.

'A perfect fit,' said Mrs Marsh.

Poor Mary was looking very plain, thought Barbara irrelevantly.

*   *   *

Mary was tired – so tired she felt she would crumble to ash at a touch, like a burnt message. Perhaps the Grim Reaper was after her in earnest now. Death had kept very close all year – taken Robin, friends, aunts, a cousin. Even the Pope had died twice that year. It had been like autumn for people.

'I get very tired,' she said decisively to Seb and Sam. She didn't think they would want to follow her into her room and make conversation, but it was as well to be on the safe side.

Seb sat down in an armchair in the little front room, and Sam idled about the kitchen and hallway. All three people on the ground floor wondered with varying degrees of desperation how they were to survive the next few days.

'Don't touch, Sam darling,' said his grandmother, coming downstairs.

Sam moved away from the arched and illuminated recess with its glass shelves of treasures – china shepherdesses, little bowls and netsuké – and they edged round each other.

'Why don't you go for a run in the Close before it gets dark?' suggested Mrs Marsh. 'Call on Evelyn and she'll show you her alligator.'

She had no hope at all that Sam would do this and so wasn't surprised when he didn't. 'Go and unpack your things,' she said. 'You're sleeping in the same room as your father.'

No one but Kate was entirely pleased with the sleeping arrangements, but Sam was horrified. He was shy of looking at his father. Knowledge of the Thrush hung between them like soiled sheets.

'Shleep on de shofa,' he offered.

'Certainly not,' said Mrs Marsh, who had just replaced the still immaculate Tudor print covers with a rather cooler pattern of cream roses on a green ground to match the carpet.

'Shleep on de floor,' said Sam hopelessly.

'Don't be silly, Sam. There are two very comfortable beds in that room and you'll sleep in one of them.' She was glad she'd had daughters. Boys were too difficult.

*　　　*　　　*

The evening passed off quietly enough. It started early with a simple supper of omelettes and peas and toast, followed by stewed apricots and cream, which they all ate standing up in the kitchen, except for Mary and Seb, who had theirs on trays in the back and front rooms respectively. Sebastian had a little stilton too, out of a jar – an early Christmas present to a lady at the W.I., who hadn't liked it at all and had passed it on to Mrs Marsh, knowing that she would have a man staying over the holiday.

Sebastian took his papers to the pub. Sam lay in the front room and watched television. Evelyn came across for company, and they all crowded into the kitchen and made the mince pies.

Mary thought about what Sam would doubtless describe as 'birf 'n' deaf'. Robin's death, the sudden absolute cessation of vaulting, joyful life, seemed to her quite as astonishing and worthy of remark as that other more widely acclaimed and admired miracle, birth. Despite her anger, she thought that God deserved more notice for this extraordinary trick. Even inclined as she was to side in rebellion with the Son of the Morning, she couldn't but praise God for his infinite invention. It was as funny, that sudden shocking silence, as Jack in the Box, a sleight-of-hand performed by a master.

*   *   *

Mrs Marsh felt strange the next morning, coming into the hallway through the front door instead of down the stairs, taking off her coat and gloves before she made a cup of tea. The tea she had drunk at Evelyn's had been wishy-washy. Her egg had been

67

under-cooked, and she had had to scrape her spoon surreptitiously with her nail before using it. Evelyn didn't rinse the washing up, and her sink and draining board were faintly scummed with dirt. She was the only slovenly resident in the Close – but also, allowed Mrs Marsh, the kindest, in spite of her irritating ways.

Mrs Marsh hoped briefly that the bed had been aired, and set about putting her own kitchen to rights. Barbara or Kate had left the washing-up brush on the wrong side of the sink and the teapot on the draining board instead of the shelf above the fridge. Remedying these little errors, she began her annual litany aloud. 'Sprouts . . .' she recited. 'Chestnuts, sausages, extra bread, extra milk, nutmeg, cloves, cinnamon, eggs, lentils, enough potatoes, enough sherry . . .'

She paused as Barbara came into the kitchen. 'Hello, darling . . . Peas, coffee, onions, chocolate, preserved ginger . . . brown sugar . . . cornflour . . . cream . . .'

Mary, lying awake next door, could visualise her mother, thumbnail hitched under her top teeth, squinting concentratedly at the shelves of the kitchen cabinet. 'Enough salt, brandy for the pudding . . .' She'd forgotten something. There was a muted shriek and a scurry. 'Barbara,' she said, 'I've got no sponge fingers and no glacé cherries for the trifle . . . oh.'

'I'll get them,' said Barbara, sharing her mother's serious appraisal of the deficiency, 'and I'll get some more butter and some biscuits, in case we run out

68

of bread, and some crumpets for tea time and some mushrooms for breakfast. Have you got cloves?'

*　　*　　*

Sam rose astonishingly early for him and left the house at midday before his mother and Kate returned from the shops.

'Goinasee a frien',' he told his grandmother nonchalantly.

'All right, dear,' she said without thinking, as she peeled chestnuts, hot from boiling water.

'Where's Sam?' asked the returned Barbara as she pulled off Kate's woolly hat and removed her own sheepskin coat.

'Gonna – gone to see a friend,' said Mrs Marsh, realising simultaneously that Sam had no friends in Innstead.

'He's gone to London,' said Barbara in a fright. Sam had friends in London – the children of Seb's publisher. They were awful, with spiky hair and pink eyes. Hunter had once brought them down for the day to give his boss a bit of a rest. She had been pleased until they arrived, thinking a publisher's children would be nice friends for hers. She had had such a shock. They wore black plastic clothes hung with steel chains and had all perfected the use of the glottal stop.

'I'll ring Hunter,' she said, conscious even through her panic of pleasure at the thought of speaking to him.

'Why?' asked Mrs Marsh puzzled.

'Because . . .' began Barbara. 'Oh never mind. Sam's gone to see Seb's publisher's children.' It sounded so respectable, spoken aloud. 'He's Hunter's boss.'

'That's nice,' said Mrs Marsh.

'If he's not back by five I'll ring Hunter then,' said Barbara, calming a little. She didn't want to appear hysterical to Hunter: frail and unjustly treated, yes — but not a nuisance.

She rang the office at five, but Hunter had left. She rang his house, but he hadn't got back yet. Having drinks with some literary woman, she thought savagely, while I'm out of my mind with worry.

Sam returned at seven. And when he did, his hair was green.

'Aaargh,' said Barbara, quite unaffectedly, as she opened the door and the outside light shone on him.

Mrs Marsh tottered back, her hands to her mouth, realising, not for the first time, that it was quite possible thoroughly to dislike one's grandchildren for the trouble and pain they caused one's own child.

'S'a fash'n,' said Sam complacently.

'It looks very Christmassy,' said Mary.

'Sebastian,' called Barbara. '*Sebastian*.' When the door of the front room remained closed, she opened it herself and thrust her verdant-haired son through it. '*Look*,' she said. 'Look what he's done. He's dyed his hair green.'

Sebastian glanced up from his papers. He found

70

his wife's twitching face far more irritating than his son's green head. He looked a little disgusted but merely remarked that it would doubtless grow out if it didn't rot, and requested everyone to be quiet as he was trying to work.

'But . . .' said Barbara, gasping, and after a while, as she still stood there, he got up and closed the door in her face.

Mrs Marsh watched quietly, admitting to herself that she found her son-in-law loathsome. She even went in to speak to him and was treated to the faint weasel gleam of his smile. 'Barbara worries too much about the children,' he told her.

Mrs Marsh stared speechlessly at his pale face, his gold-rimmed spectacles and his pale hair. His head looked as though it had been lightly buttered – so sleek, so unguent and so slight. He made her think of hard roads under a film of rain, shallow and dangerous; of slugs and Nazis and the minister she sometimes met in the terminal ward of the cancer hospital when she was arranging the flowers . . .

Mrs Marsh crossed the hallway – two steps – to Mary's room. 'He leaves too much to Barbara,' she said. 'He never gives her a thought. He's wrapped up in his work.'

'He's all right,' said Mary inadequately. 'Barbara worries too much.' He had to have some defence, she thought, against her sister's grasping, tentacular nervousness.

Mrs Marsh sighed, remembering, for no reason, a moment when Barbara was a little baby sitting on her knee in the springtime at Melys y Bwyd and Mary was dancing — a silly two-year-old's dance. Suddenly someone had laughed and laughed until the room was full of laughter, and it was the little baby on her knee — who previously had only smiled, or cried — laughing with the utmost delight at the dancing child.

'I don't believe he loves her,' she said.

Mary recoiled. 'I'm sure he does,' she said with artificial formality.

But Mrs Marsh doubted it. She wondered crossly if anyone but she knew what it was to love — how painful and tiring it could be. She wondered how Mary had loved Robin. She remembered how Robin had loved Mary, bounding at a photograph of her as a girl crying 'Isn't she lovely? Isn't she beautiful?', leaping through the door, not stopping to say hullo. Such extravagant behaviour. She wished she could tell Mary how much *she* loved her, but Mary wouldn't listen . . .

She got up tiredly. She could cope with anything if people would be happy, would make an effort. Really, it seemed as if only she held all her world together. 'I wish you'd speak to Sebastian,' she said without hope. 'He'd listen to you.' It was Mary's fault that Barbara had met Seb, though she'd been pleased at the time.

'It's snowing again,' said Mary. There would be no point in trying to explain to her mother that the most ruthless dictators, impalers, people who put people in sacks and threw them in the river, robbers, politicians – all, all have always considered those who offer them the mildest hint of criticism to be extremely wicked and deserving of annihilation.

'He wouldn't listen,' she said.

*　　*　　*

Sam was very good that evening. He smiled several times and jovially shoved Kate with his elbow when she mentioned poetry. He seemed quite unselfconscious about his hair, not even glancing in the numerous mirrors from time to time as anyone else might have done, for pleasure or reassurance, and helped his grandmother get the tree out from the cupboard under the stairs. Mrs Marsh never had a real tree. The needles were so difficult to remove from the carpet. She kept a number of little golden nets, put tangerines in them, and hung them on the ringer, interspersed with realistic-looking birds made from *papier mâché* and feathers. The effect, though artificial, was preferable to the garish pyramids of light in the neighbours' windows. Mrs Marsh had no paper chains, balls or lanterns, just some real holly that the greengrocer acquired from somewhere on the downs. She strung her Christmas cards around the hall and put chrysanthemums in the front room. But she thought Mary's room looked bleak for the time of year with no decorations at all.

'Put up your cards,' she urged. 'It looks so miserable.'

'No,' said Mary. She liked the pale walls and the

firelight and the skeleton garden visible through the window, unrivalled by brief baubles. And she disliked the funereal opulence of Christmas, the anxious overeating of a cold people in midwinter, the forced gaiety and the absurd expense. Christmas should be looking forward to spring, the thin clear light and the rains of hope, not banging and whistling in uncertain rebellion against the frozen despair of present dearth.

Mrs Marsh peered through the window. 'It's snowing quite heavily now. I wonder if I've got enough caster sugar.'

*   *   *

'Ba,' said Mrs Marsh on the morning of Christmas eve. 'We must get some more fruit. I think Sam's been eating it.'

Sam didn't like fruit. Kate had been eating it. But Barbara didn't think it worth explaining.

'Don't take the car,' said Mrs Marsh. 'Put on your boots and wrap up warmly and walk in the soft snow on the edges – the roads are like glass. Just get oranges and apples and nuts – I've got bananas in the cupboard. They had some nice pineapples the other day but the price was disgusting. If you take Sam,' she said as an afterthought, 'make sure he wears something on his head.'

Sam stayed behind. He sat on a stool in Mary's room and stared blankly before him. There was nothing she could say, since he obviously couldn't

74

sit with Seb and his papers, his grandmother didn't approve of people sitting around in their bedrooms and Innstead offered nothing to divert him. He sat silently in her place by the window, his legs stretched out and his long feet in black boots falling sideways like a supine rabbit's. The light from the garden shone coldly on his beige skin and his green hair, and he slid lower, his back against the wall, as the birds went on scrapping just outside. In imagination he straddled the rooftree like a warlock. Lines of silent, gape-mouthed people came to stare at him, and he knocked all their heads off, one by one, with superbly aimed sharp-edged slates, which he unhooked from their moorings with professional ease. (He knew how to do this since a holiday at Melys y Bwyd, when a man had replaced all the slates blown off by a wicked Welsh gale and he had sat on an upstairs windowsill, his back to the hills, and watched him all one morning. They had called from below, 'Oh Sam, do be careful. You'll fall.' But they hadn't dared go into the room for fear of startling him. The slater hadn't minded him at all – just kept on doing his job and humming.) Zing went the slates, slicing through the winter air, decapitating people – none of whom were known to Sam: anonymous, complaisant game. They kept on wandering into view until the air was full of their silly heads, flying around as thick as autumn leaves. His brief cheerfulness had gone.

Mary watched him warily. He was, she realised, full of something and likely to confide in her. Several people had recently told her things that they would prefer not to be widely known, confirming her in her suspicion that they too thought she was going to die. Sometimes Sam reminded her of Robin, and she couldn't be sure whether she liked him for this or whether she would prefer to see him dead too.

'Dad's got a mistress,' Sam announced at last in perfect English.

Mrs Marsh, passing through the hall, heard him clearly and stood still, her hand suddenly cold on the newel post.

'She shings,' added Sam irrelevantly.

'Well?' asked Mary.

''orrible,' said Sam. 'In 'er chest.'

'A contralto, I should think,' mused Mary. 'I'm glad we got that clear.'

Sam was greatly relieved to see how little his aunt cared. She didn't love anyone enough to mind at all what they did. He thought there was a lot to be said for people devoid of passion, and in Mary passion had dwindled to one desire – that she might see Robin again – and one fear – that she might not. Sam wasn't to know this, but whatever the reason his aunt's distant coldness was a relief after the heated curiosity of his mother who anguishedly loved and disapproved of him.

Mrs Marsh peered round the door. She knew perfectly well that she ought to go on upstairs to the lavatory, as she had intended, and say nothing of what she had overheard, but she couldn't help herself.

'Are you telling lies, Sam?' she demanded.

Sam blushed. 'Nah,' he said indignantly – like all liars, far more offended than the usually veracious at having one of his few truthful utterances doubted.

Mrs Marsh glared at him with the wholly unfair dislike reserved for the bearers of evil tidings. It would be better, thought Mary, if such people were made to wear distinctive clothing, so that the archers could shoot them down before they reached the barricades to upset the embattled inhabitants. There was seldom anything to be gained from the premature reception of bad news.

Sam, too, was angry. He thought old people shouldn't listen at doors and was aware again of the hopeless impossibility of reprimanding his seniors. Surrounded by moral turpitude, he yet knew that any word of rebuke from him would be considered impertinent, naughty and asking for trouble. Zing-split, he went in his head, mowing down the incessant ranks of imagined strangers – but it would be better, he suddenly realised, if his grandmother didn't believe him, for she certainly cared. She smelt of love and worry.

Mrs Marsh had reached the same conclusion. 'You talk a terrible lot of nonsense,' she told Sam, running upstairs. 'Don't encourage him, Mary.' She had just noticed an extraordinary family resemblance between aunt and nephew, and fumed briefly at the unfairness of things. After all, there were countless other relations Sam could have taken after . . .

*　　*　　*

Throughout the afternoon neighbours kept calling with heavily wrapped small offerings of marmalade and bath-salts, which were added to the pile round the tree. They all knew Mary, and many of these things were for her; but Mary lurked in her room and left it to her mother to hand round the decorative boxes of matches and the apple-shaped candles which she had got for her to give in reciprocation. Her mother had had to wrap all these presents herself since Mary was loth to wind any material round anything or put anything in boxes and it hadn't been necessary to buy a present for Robin. Christmas wasn't necessary for Mary. She would wait for Easter and that other unanswerable feat of godly legerdemain. Resurrection, after all, was the *pièce de résistance,* deserving only of the roll of drums, the fanfare, the held breath – making the miracle of birth and even death quite commonplace.

Evelyn, as best friend, kept her visit and her gift till last – until the evening, when she saw the lights go on. Then, glowing with the selfless pride of the donor, she crossed the Close to claim her reward of gratitude and a glass of sherry.

'You can't really wrap it up and put it under the tree,' she said, 'but I thought I'd bring it over tonight so it can settle in before the rush tomorrow.'

'What is it?' enquired Mrs Marsh, deeply suspicious. Evelyn was scatter-brained, and anything could be hidden under her cloak. She should have been warned when Evelyn had said that she had 'just the present' for Mary. It was bound to be something totally unsuitable.

Evelyn knelt, fumbling under her cloak, and placed her gift on the floor. It staggered about, no more pleased to be given than Mrs Marsh was to receive it. It shrank and spat and sniffled without hope at the bleach-washed floor.

'Kitty, kitty,' said Evelyn, crouching lower to address it. 'I found it on the downs three days ago,' she explained, 'all on its lonesome, crying under a bush, and I kept it in the shed so you wouldn't see it.'

'It's wild,' said Mrs Marsh.

'No, it isn't,' said Evelyn. 'It *was* when I found it, but it's got used to me now. It sits on my lap.'

'House-trained?' asked Mrs Marsh.

'Nearly,' said Evelyn offhandedly, stroking the hostile kitten as it tried to hide under the kitchen cabinet.

Mrs Marsh was very cross. She had a chaotic vision of half-eaten birds, cat mess, hairs and future generations of kittens all over the house and garden.

'Its mother is probably looking everywhere for it,' she said spitefully. 'Parent animals leave their young concealed while they go foraging for food.'

Evelyn grew stubborn. 'It was lost,' she said. 'It was all thin, and its nose was bleeding.'

'Well, I'd better find it a box,' said Mrs Marsh resignedly. 'Come on, puss.' It was a tiny brindled thing, much too young to be seeking its fortune alone.

'You have to put its milk on your finger,' said Evelyn, not looking at her friend, 'and let it lick it, and then put your finger in its saucer until it starts lapping. And you have to squash a little bit of sardine in milk, and it eats that for its dinner off your finger.'

Mrs Marsh was outraged. Did Evelyn really suppose that she had time to sit around hand-feeding cats?

'It's Mary's cat,' said Evelyn. 'She'll do it.'

Mrs Marsh doubted it, but had discerned Evelyn's purpose. The kitten was to give Mary an interest, a reason for living. This was a common theme in women's magazines and the afternoon films on television — except that it was usually a child, physically or mentally afflicted, who was restored to the world by the love of a dumb animal.

'Is it a boy or a girl?' she asked. 'We'll have to have it seen to.'

'I think it's a girl,' said Evelyn, brightening. 'It's very affectionate.' The kitten backed away from her, its mouth open in silent loathing.

'I've got a ribbon to put round its neck, and a card,' said Evelyn, 'so I'll come round in the morning and put them on.' She was a little disappointed at Mrs Marsh's lack of enthusiasm and wondered uneasily whether she would appreciate the painting of the lunatic asylum seen through the branches of a laburnum tree that was to be her own present.

'Have a sherry,' said Mrs Marsh at last, taking pity on her friend's downcast mien.

'It'll be good for Mary,' said Evelyn. 'It'll give her something else to think about.' It was her contention that the bereaved grew ill from grief. 'Take widows,' she said. 'They all either get cancer or take to drink.'

'I didn't,' Mrs Marsh pointed out.

Evelyn looked rather knowing – perhaps thinking it was early days yet. 'You're very unusual,' she said patronisingly.

But Mrs Marsh reluctantly inclined more to Mary's theory, the arsy-versy of 'nothing succeeds like success', that if a person is born with a hare-lip he will undoubtedly go on to develop short sight and flat feet.

She sighed, and turned on the wireless to listen to the news. It was preceded by a talk from an Anglican bishop.

'What does Christmas mean to *you*, Bishop?' enquired the wireless.

The bishop began, 'Oh, a time when families get together, chip each other, pull each other's leg . . .'

The words drifted through the wall.

'And of course,' the bishop went on, 'it's a religious time, and it's when one has a bit of a rest and wonders what life is all about. Life is a strange mixture of sadness and joy, isn't it?' he observed, his tone deepening. 'I went to have a drink with some of the clergy . . .' He laughed. 'Har har! And I said morning service in my own chapel with my grandmother present, and then I went to one of the large London prisons, and then to an Intensive Care Unit. Then at an Old Persons' Home I sat down at the piano and played "I'm Tired and I Want to Go Home". Har har!' The bishop's tone, which had lightened, now deepened again. 'I am a poorer man today,' he announced, 'because there are poor people on the street. *But* – love is stronger than hate even on the streets of Belfast.'

In a pig's arse, thought Mary.

She and Sam glanced at each other, embarrassed. 'Dear me,' she said.

The wireless emitted a final self-satisfied holy giggle and some distant well-trained children began to sing carols.

*   *   *

The snow melted again overnight, leaving everyone with a sense of anti-climax which conflicted awkwardly with their expectations of Christmas Day. It was mild and grey and wet, and no one really enjoyed the early breakfast of mushrooms and bacon. Not even the bottle of champagne they drank as they opened their presents did much to raise their spirits. Nor did their presents.

Sebastian announced that he had left Barbara's bottle of scent in his rooms and she'd have to wait for it until they got home, and Barbara instantly and irrationally believed he'd given it to the Thrush.

'He's teasing you, Mummy,' Kate said. 'Daddy, show her what we got.'

'You show her,' said Sebastian, settling back in his chair and folding his hands across the green cardigan that covered the beginnings of a paunch. His eyes were invisible behind the steely shine of his spectacles, his skin as fair and smooth as a baby's. Mrs Marsh felt her mouth twist with distaste.

For Barbara they had got an embroidered ethnic evening bag, hung with tassels and gleaming with bits of mirror. She recognised it at once and wondered remotely whether she would find a slice of turkey in it.

'We got it in the boutique,' cried Kate. 'Oh, Mummy, isn't it perfectly exquisite.'

'Yes,' said Barbara, sense returning as she realised that these things were widely available. Still, she wondered again, whether her husband was stupid or cruel, and wished, dully despairing, that he was neither.

Evelyn came across at mid-morning with her ribbon and card and proceeded to drive the kitten — who had spent a pleasant night on an old jumper and was beginning to relax — mad.

'Do hold it, Kate,' she implored, as it tried to turn itself inside out.

'You'll throttle the damn thing in a minute,' said Mrs Marsh impatiently. 'Just give her the kitten and the card separately.'

It wasn't what Evelyn had planned. Separated, the kitten and the blue satin ribbon weren't nearly as appealing, but there was nothing else for it.

Mary thanked her formally and patted the kitten before it went to ground under her bed. It emerged later when she was alone again and played for a while in an unpractised fashion. She wished it no harm.

Mrs Marsh listened devotedly to the Queen's broadcast.

The monarch let it be known that, among other things, it would give her, personally, much pleasure if people would stop killing each other. (Her son had recently made several uninformed and ill-advised comments on church matters, freedom of expression and the management of industry, while her consort frequently exhorted his wife's subjects to pull out their fingers, cease their bloody-mindedness, get off their backsides, and so on, in a simple, sailor-manly fashion.)

It would be better, thought Mary, if they were all to keep their jaws clamped firmly shut on the silver spoons with which they were born for the purpose. Or alternatively they might get the authors of the animal books to write their scripts for them. (The heir already spoke of elephants as 'heffalumps'.)

In each home in the Close the inhabitants, like Mrs Marsh, would be avidly lapping up these banalities. People who believed in monarchy, reflected Mary, were certifiably mad – madder than people who believed in little fat gurus or addressed their prayers to Elvis Presley. She looked aside as the high gentle voice delivered a final, deplorably limp and unleavened platitude.

'Well, she can't be controversial,' said Mrs Marsh, observing her daughter's expression. 'You haven't been to church for ages,' she added, taking the offensive. Both her children had been brought up in their father's faith, but she herself had never converted and Barbara had naturally lapsed when she married Sebastian.

Her mother's train of thought satisfied Mary that she was right in estimating that the belief in monarchy was religious in character rather than secular and patriotic.

'I'll get Father Whatsit to pop in and see you later this week,' Mrs Marsh said rather threateningly.

'All right,' said Mary placidly. She wasn't an enthusiast. She was resigned to faith rather than a believer, having no doubts – no doubts, that is, as to the existence of God. Of his mood, his intentions, she wasn't sure. She saw no reason to suppose that he meant her well in the accepted meaning of that term. He didn't, as her mother did, wish her a nice house, a nice husband, nice children, a well-trained pet, happiness, longevity and a sherry in the evenings. Nor did she want any of these things. She sometimes thought he might have left her Robin, but that wasn't his way. Her anger stopped short of God and was sustained by her hatred of death and the little demons in whom she saw herself reflected: destructive, gleeful, purple-tongued and bloody-mouthed – eternally mindless and beyond appeal. There was no point in fearing these unpleasant little gods since she knew they were subject to the limits of her consciousness and would never make it across the wilderness. Even Death, the jaunty jester-king, would flag before he reached the end of the wilderness. God was beyond the wilderness, but God without Robin was not enough and Mary, like an abandoned dog, couldn't decide whether to stay in life, where she had last seen her darling, or to set off in pursuit.

* * *

Sebastian, Barbara and Kate went for a walk, surprising everybody with this evidence of family solidarity. Barbara wanted to clear her head before Hunter arrived. She had begun, inevitably, to wonder, as the time approached, whether her dreams were capable of realisation. Would *The Bear,* for instance, be open on Christmas Day? Would Hunter invite her to accompany him to *The Bear?* Did he even know of its existence? Could she suggest that he accompany her? Hardly. She began to construct a new fantasy in which all her family went for a walk – Mary could go to sleep – leaving Hunter time to begin to woo her. That would be enough to start with. The thought of illicit sexual congress in the Close made her nervous. A glance, a touch, would be enough, thought starving Barbara, sweating slightly in her sheepskin in the damp dull day.

Sebastian said nothing. He muttered occasionally, but not of his mistress. He was thinking of his work. Kate, at her most determinedly winsome, gambolled. She picked leaves and remarked on their symmetry; she nibbled berries and made faces; she pointed out features on the houses that they passed and recited bits of poetry. Even Barbara began to find her annoying and to wish she had left her behind. But it wasn't impossible that Mrs Marsh and Evelyn would also leave the house and that Kate, her ewe lamb, would be alone with Mary. In Barbara's mind her sister had taken on a mythic, fairy-tale quality, a witch-like aspect, step-motherly, greedy and cruel. Because surely, she muddled, anyone so bitterly bereft must be dangerous. It was true that Mary had within her-self that ill-will which only the primitive fully under-stand that the dead bear to the living. She was spoiled as the raped, or the dead themselves, are spoiled – changed beyond all chance of worldly repair – but not dangerous. She didn't care enough about any-thing to be dangerous.

*   *   *

Mary had offered to do the sprouts, since there seemed to be no reason why she shouldn't.

'You don't need to cut crosses on their bottoms,' said her mother, gasping for breath as she flew about. 'I found out years ago it isn't necessary.'

'Oh good,' said Mary.

Evelyn caught Mrs Marsh by the sleeve as she sped past. 'This is the first Christmas since—' she said in a spraying hiss.

Mrs Marsh stared at her.

'Since – *you* know.'

Evelyn shrugged meaningfully at Mary, who was listening. When the elderly grew deaf they never seemed to realise that their condition wasn't universal.

87

'It's not natural,' said Evelyn. 'She should break down.'

Mrs Marsh was inclined to agree with her, but wasn't prepared to say so. 'Well, she wouldn't do it now,' she said. 'She's far too considerate.'

They all knew this to be untrue.

Mary smiled down on the sprouts. No one understood that she was incapable of grieving sufficiently for Robin, whose death had seemed so preposterously catastrophic that all the acceptedly appropriate reactions were inadequate. The advice, commonly offered, that she should give herself up to it and just let go, struck her as incomparably fatuous. She bore herself with care, like a glass already singing which would shatter at a touch; and she smiled quite often, for it was useless to deny that the situation had its humorous side. There had, after all, been only one little death.

Evelyn was basting the turkey. Mrs Marsh wished she wouldn't as she was never quite sure that Evelyn had washed her hands, but it was impossible to stop people helping if they really wanted to.

*   *   *

By midday Mrs Marsh had performed prodigies of tidying. All the crumpled wrapping and boxes were in a sack, and the tangerine peel and half-eaten chocolates had been safely gathered up. The little tables in the front room were laid ready, crowded and festive with the best mats and table napkins, scarlet crackers and centre-pieces of silvered holly. Avocado pears laved in oil and lemon juice stood in special little dishes on the kitchen cabinet, and the potatoes, ready for roasting, gleamed whitely through the water in a blue saucepan.

The time had come, they considered for a sherry.

Mary shuddered. So much food. The little gods fed on human blood – those dark gods in whom joy and sorrow, good and evil, mercy and malice were as irredeemably mixed as the breadcrumbs, onion, sausage, sage and celery in the force for the turkey. But they were, she assured herself, merely a mark of man's confusion, a symbol of that gloomy theory, the Second Law of Thermodynamics, which suggests that all construction, movement, endeavour merely hasten that time when the world and all its works will be utterly undone, a whirling mass of dust in an infinite desolation.

There had been another feast once, a long time ago . . . in Melys y Bwyd . . . in the time of the old people, the dream time . . . It had become an anti-feast, a reversal of the Law, a kind of resurrection – irritating alike to the hungry and to the rational.

Mary closed her eyes . . .

*   *   *

A number of ladies and gentlemen had sat down in a high chamber with a great fire, and since they had fasted through Advent they longed for the feast to start and looked hungrily at the middle of the board

89

where stood a wooden charger bearing a roast en-gastered swan, the erstwhile lord of the lake. Within this swan were concealed other birds, each containing one smaller. And at the very centre of all, where once had been the swan's liver, was a wren's egg, boiled.

The master of the feast had just raised his knife when a cold wind swung through the hall, drifting and swirling the smoke and making it plain that someone had opened the door. As all the expected guests were present this could only be a traveller, who must be invited to join the feast. It was not only the draught that chilled the company, for they were *very* hungry and all peered through the cloudy dimness of the hall to make sure that there was only one traveller to accommodate. Sometimes bands of pilgrims came by, cockle-shelled, flat-hatted and sandalled, telling tales of foreign lands where there lived men who had fathered one son and possessed only one milch goat for the sustenance of that child, and who when visited by strangers, even were those strangers hostile, slew the innocent goat to entertain them. The feasters were not yet so far advanced in civilisation that they could afford to laugh too heartily at such tales, and no one wished at this moment to be put to the test.

Most were reassured to see a single figure approach and to know by the haggard features, the threadbare garments and the evil smell that this was a holy person, accustomed to frugality. Some, more worldly wise than the rest, thought bleakly that this holy person might well consume more of the feast than the invited guests together.

The master bade him sit, and all were relieved to see him place his hands each in the opposite sleeve. Even then, long before anyone had heard of the germ theory of disease, no one wished to see his filthy hands dipped in the communal dish, and each looked surreptitiously to see if he carried the short knife necessary to spike the pieces of meat that were placed on each person's manchet. Even the servants who sat below the salt, and for whom the bread was eventually destined, raised their chilled bottoms slightly from the bench to look anxiously at the holy person and wonder about his table manners.

He had a cold grey gaze when his hood was back, and his head was very bony.

On his right sat the sweet-faced lady with the white hair, who smiled at him kindly and was good enough not to fear the lice that were even now calculating the distance between him and her in their own determination to survive – for he had grown hopelessly thin and juiceless. He is one of those who range the wilderness, she thought approvingly, living on nuts and berries and the roots that only such people know of. A holy, holy person.

'Tell us a story,' she asked, knowing that such good people, starved and sanctified, were implicit with wisdom.

He was silent, and the sweet-faced lady picked at her manchet with her thin fingers before turning to the man on her right. That man, angered at the incivility of the holy person, leaned before the sweet-faced lady and said, '*I pray you tell us a story*', his hand on the hilt of the knife he used to settle arguments. He was already in a bad, nervous frame of mind because he feared that the Prince of his district thought he was growing too powerful and was plotting his destruction. In the end, he knew, the Prince would prevail, since the Prince's people had ruled these few acres from time immemorial and the warrior himself came of foreign stock. In the small hours of the cold ill-smelling nights he would lie awake wondering whether he could elect to die by the Blood Eagle as his forebears in similar case had done. In those days before the invention of aspirin, gas ovens, plastic bags, this form of euthanasia involved the willing co-operation of the victim who, lying face down, would consent to have his ribs sprung from his backbone and his heart removed. Although brave, the warrior often wondered how much this would hurt and whether it would not be wiser to permit the Prince's heavies to club or spear or garotte him to death. It was a matter of pride and a difficult problem to resolve. He had heard a raven croaking in an inauspicious manner only that morning – the raven whose image rode high on his coat of arms, dominating the scallions rampant on a field argent. The warrior felt himself surrounded by treachery and scowled threateningly at the impertinent holy person.

The sweet-faced lady patted his leather-clad arm. '*Aquila non captat muscas*,' she told him in a reassuring whisper. 'Eagles don't catch flies.' (Her chaplain had been reading to her from ancient books (the tenth book of Pliny was his favourite) and her head was stuffed with foolish saws and a mass of error.)

The holy person laughed, an unpleasant sound. He spoke.

'God's angels have a keen nose for prayer,' he said.

The guests smiled and relaxed a little, thinking that this was a witless holy person – there were many such – since they all knew that God and his angels had *ears* for prayer.

But the holy person continued. 'The angels in Heaven,' he said, 'when they smell the prayers rising from the mouths of the righteous to the throne of God, cry: "Oh God, be still. Do not reply, let us breathe in that delectable breath. Oh God, be silent. Oooohh, ahh . . ." But when the unrighteous pray, then "Oh," cry the angels, "this stench is insupportable. Dear God, answer that prayer at once or we will fall from your heaven like poisoned wasps. Dear God, we implore you, give them what they desire or their foul breath will make us sick." And so . . .' continued the holy person composedly, 'as I am on the side of the angels I will show you a story.'

Most of the guests merely reflected, a little bewilderedly now, that stories were to be *heard,* but the man on the right of the sweet-faced lady who, although a warrior, was no fool, rose, his face contused with the blood of rage.

'Black, blasphemous, nameless, mannerless outsider . . .' he began.

93

He stopped. For the holy person had stretched out his skinny hand over the board, had directed the gaze of his cold grey eyes at the centre and was plainly, although quite motionless, up to something.

There was a stirring in the depths of the swan, a mild, gentle, barely perceptible stirring, and out from its vent rolled the wren's egg. It moved just a little, to and fro. There was a minute sound, a crack like the tiny cracking of a sprig of heather responding to the first spring sunshine. The shell broke, and out – with a movement between a hop and a stagger – came a wren chick.

'Oh, how enchanting,' cried the ladies.

But the sweet-faced lady was first. She picked it up, very carefully, and broke off a corner of her manchet. She hollowed it out and put the chick in it and pulled out a little of her white hair to line the sides of the exposed crust.

All were spellbound, even the angry man. The tale of this trick would enliven many another banquet. All present planned to feast out on it for months to come, saying to the sceptical: 'There were many of us there. You can ask so and so, and so and so, if you don't believe me – and so and so . . .'

But the holy person's story was not over. Suddenly he flung up his left hand, stiff-fingered, and a shower of dry dead skin fell to the table.

The swan heaved slightly, and out came a scorched, plucked, mutilated, part-melted coot. It complained and fluttered blindly and nakedly, until the holy person stretched out his long arm and anointed it with a smear of grease and gravy from the dish – whereupon, restored, it flapped into a pitcher of ale and splashed contentedly.

'A joke is a joke . . .' said the warrior, who by now desperately wanted his dinner and could see it diminishing in a wholly unnatural fashion; 'but this has gone far enow.'

It was quite useless. The holy person, it seemed, was enjoying himself.

The sauce – the lovely thick, succulent sauce – was gone. The cows in the byres lowed with astonishment as their udders filled instantly with warm milk faintly onion-flavoured. The swarthy inhabitants of Pamplona were astounded to discover a full crop of almonds on a picked tree on the day of Christ's nativity. Being human, they had to have a reason for everything, and so they attributed this miracle to the piety of the recently repentant town whore who had developed thrush – called in those days St Cunno's fire after a certain saint, coeval with these events. (He had found an abandoned nest. The parent bird (a storm petrel named for St Peter because it seemed to the observer in the days before binoculars that these birds walked on water) had been killed by local fishermen, who thought it was the spirit of a piratical lord from the mainland who had regularly demanded the catch and ravaged the settlements on the island each autumn, leaving the few inhabitants to face near death from starvation until they had drowned him by sneakily holing his boat. The saint had lit a small smouldering fire of sea-wrack and eglantine in the rock below and had himself crouched, legs akimbo, over the eggs in the teeth of the raging Atlantic gales until the nestlings hatched.) The whore had abandoned her calling to spend her nights flat out on the cathedral steps. She couldn't sleep anyway, she was so uncomfortable. She died in a traffic accident quite soon after that, on the day they were running the bulls, being much too tired to skip out of the way – and in the course of time they canonised her.

The onions were back, safely entombed in the ice-bound earth. The herbs shivered in the Christmas air. The currants, undesiccated, unwrinkled, gleamed in their dark pristine grapeness on the slopes of Agadir, where the natives marvelled briefly at the mercy of Allah and carried on as usual. The spices were back in the souks of Samarkand, the honey back in the comb. Even the spiteful cook's spit returned to his mouth as he was speaking evil of his master in the down-house, surprising him exceedingly as it was still boiling-hot from the sauce boat. The flour on its way back to the wheatfield was winnowed again by the wind and blew away with the snow.

In the great hall the master, the warrior and most of the guests had fallen asleep, now half-stunned, half-bored by this impossible happening. When they awoke they would say they had dreamed.

The sweet-faced lady with the white hair still watched. A pigeon had followed the coot on to the table, immaculately wrapped as for Ascot. (How the guests would have enjoyed Ascot had they been born in a later age!) A hen, indignant as hens often are, strutted the board as one seeking somewhere to lodge a complaint. A duck – a worthy duck, fat and bosomy, since he had been the lady's pet and each day ate white wheaten bread from her fingers – golloped the water from the warrior's beaker. A heron, a widgeon, a bustard, a crane stood around preening the last traces of their once-cooked blood and gravy from their offended feathers. Bird droppings lay everywhere and the hall was taking on the characteristic odour of the aviary.

And at last, the swan, the lord of the lake, cast from his beak the gilded quince which had held it agape, tossed from his head the crown of gingerbread, threw from his wings the wreaths of thyme and flung himself with majestic ease into the smoke-laden air of the rafters.

The smoke dispersed, the hall door swung open with the mighty draught. The birds flew. The swan, before he left, with one beat of his great wings broke the right leg of the sweet-faced lady with the white hair, and then was gone to the water. He had forgotten to tear from his splendid throat the necklace of dried peppercorns, and to this day on that lake are to be seen swans with speckled necks . . . The duck never recovered his trust in his mistress and refused all her blandishments. She didn't really mind, since she had been looking forward to eating him, and the sight of him sloshing around in the green pond-weed made her nervous . . .

'You'd feel so much better, Mary, if you *did* something instead of sitting there day-dreaming,' said Mrs Marsh. 'We're having lunch soon.'

The thought of the entropic delights of Christmas lunch made Mary feel sick. She could smell smoke and burned flesh. 'Something's caught,' she said, wishing the turkey could unlatch the oven door, free itself like four-and-twenty blackbirds, rise like the phoenix and go and gobble in the garden, leaving the flesh-eaters to drink snow and eat chrysanthemums.

Worms had eaten Robin. Cheek, thought Mary, outraged beyond all adequate expression. Beautiful Robin was ashes and dust and the droppings of worms.

'Oh hell,' said Mrs Marsh. 'Evelyn's turned up the oven.'

At this critical moment the telephone and doorbell rang simultaneously.

'Godfathers,' said Mrs Marsh, running out and stretching her arms cruciform to lift the receiver and open the door in the same movement.

Barbara and Kate rushed in saying 'Ooooh, it's turned so *cold*' and 'Ooooh, it's warmer in here.' They ran upstairs to put on their frocks for lunch, and Sebastian slowly divested himself of his tweed coat and hat and green woollen scarf, getting in the way of Mrs Marsh, who was growing increasingly agitated over the telephone and trying to disguise it from whomever she was speaking to.

98

'That was Hunter,' she said accusingly, having crashed down the receiver. 'He's bringing some American. His aeroplane wouldn't go last night because it's foggy. There's melting ice on the runway, the flight controllers are all on strike and they had a bomb scare at the terminal. Too many excuses. I don't think he *wanted* to go.' She stamped her foot on the parquet. 'What will he sit on?' she demanded.

'You could bring in a deckchair,' said Barbara.

'No, I couldn't,' said Mrs Marsh, who was in no mood to take advice, even from Barbara. 'Evelyn,' she called to the kitchen, 'we'll have to borrow one of your chairs. Sebastian . . .' she addressed the front room. 'Will you go with Evelyn and bring a chair back?'

'Sam will go,' said Sebastian.

'Sam,' called Mrs Marsh, 'put on a woolly hat and go with Evelyn to get a chair, or you'll have no lunch.'

'S'cold,' complained Sam, sliding downstairs on his heels. He was wearing skin-tight jeans and a tee shirt.

'Borrow your father's coat and hat,' suggested Mrs Marsh crossly. Sebastian was quite unbelievably lazy and thoughtless not to realise that it would make her position impossible if the neighbours were to clap eyes on Sam's green hair. 'Go very quickly and don't talk to anyone.'

Evelyn had been surprisingly unperturbed by Sam's hair. She wasn't a bad old soul, thought Mrs Marsh. There was something to be said for the artistic viewpoint. Evelyn, though not the most proper inhabitant of the Close – she didn't *quite* qualify for the description 'a very nice person' – nevertheless had virtues that the others lacked. There had been an evening, years ago, when Evelyn and her sister, since dead, had first arrived and Mary had been down for the weekend. Mrs Marsh had given them supper because their kitchen things were all in tea chests. 'You must stay and meet my daughter,' she had insisted; 'she's in publishing', adding silently 'and so clever and pretty' with secret, satisfied motherly contentment. Mary had been late. They were all quite happy waiting for her: Evelyn and Yvonne tired after the upheaval of moving, Mrs Marsh peaceful and proud, and complacent. When they heard the sound of the key in the lock they had all sat up, put down their coffee cups and gazed expectantly at the front-room door, eyes raised to the approximate level of a human face. But when the door opened they had had to lower their eyes because Mary had come in on all fours, head down, her hair swinging slowly back and forth. She wasn't even all that drunk, Mrs Marsh had realised furiously, noting the light of intelligence in one bright eye briefly visible and alert through swaying hair. Then Mary had gone to sleep on the floor under the window. Evelyn and her sister had been very understanding, but it had been weeks before Mrs Marsh could really like them again. Trust Mary not to go to *The Bear*. Trust Mary to go to the one disreputable pub in the district – the one with the touts and stable

100

boys and riff-raff from the city, the one by the racecourse, the one where suburbia was defined by the mingled cries of owls and drunks. Mrs Marsh wondered where the bad blood had come from. Not from her dear John. It must be from somewhere in herself, she thought, with puzzled guilt. Still, the incident had made her realise after a while the value of Evelyn's dimly perceived, but largely tolerant, view of life. And when Mary had come home with Robin, the enchanting fruit of sin, only Evelyn had said 'Oh, what a dear little baby! How sweet!' The other neighbours had been much too polite to mention it at all and had passed by on the other side.

*   *   *

It was growing late – dark in the garden and the turkey drying in the oven.

'It's nearly four,' said Mrs Marsh. 'We'll have to eat now.'

She eyed the growing array of empty bottles. It was impossible to know who had drunk what – there had been so many odds and ends of whisky, rum, vodka, martini, liqueurs in the bottom of the front-room cabinet. The sherry, too, was going down rapidly – she had bought six bottles and two had gone. Impossible, she thought, a touch bemused by her three glasses of Bristol Cream.

She looked critically at Barbara and was reassured. Barbara was wearing lipstick and a new silver belt on her crimson frock, and Mrs Marsh knew her well

101

enough to know that if she had been feeling like a deceived wife she would have dressed the part – dowdy and plain and sad. Barbara had always tried to fulfil expectations, whatever they might be. It was too ridiculous that of her two daughters one should be so biddable and the other so rebellious – even Mary's present state seemed like an act of revolt.

Mary had beaten Sam to the place by the window. She wished she were alone, and that Hunter and Mr Mauss weren't coming. She wished she could lie in the garden and come up later with the crocuses. What a rest that would be. She had lost interest in the world. A world in which Robin could die was a foolish, trivial place where nothing made sense and she had no desire to linger.

'I can hear them at the door,' said Barbara, her colour deepening.

'Oh godfathers,' said Mrs Marsh.

'Let them in,' said Mary hastily, hoping to prevent them knocking. 'You'll like Mr Mauss,' she added, to cover her brief exposure of weakness. 'He'll probably thank you for entertaining him in your lovely home.'

'It'll be nice for Seb,' said Barbara, beginning to gabble. 'He's never really had the time to see enough of his American publisher. They can have a nice long talk . . .' Her hands were wet.

'Good heavens, it's started to snow again,' announced Mrs Marsh as she opened the door. 'Come in. You must be frozen. Give me your coats. Everyone's in here. How do you do. What a nuisance about your plane. Seasonal weather. Seb, give them a drink.'

Mary and Sam sat on stolidly in the back room.

'Here's Hunter,' cried Mrs Marsh, flinging open the door and fixing Mary with an imperative, maternal eye, indicating that the moment had come to display some manners, to offer some show of vivacity. 'She's much better,' she told Hunter. 'The doctor's very pleased with her.'

But he wasn't, Mary knew. He was annoyed with her, because she didn't respond to his skills.

'Hullo, Hunter,' she said.

'And Mr Mauss,' prompted Mrs Marsh in a sing-song voice as to a class of five-year-olds.

'Hullo, Mr Mauss,' said Mary.

'That's Sam,' said Mrs Marsh, in a normal, hopeless voice, waving a hand at her grandson.

'Hi, Mary. Hi, Sam,' said Mr Mauss.

Hunter felt a little hysterical. The nursery-school atmosphere was becoming too noticeable. He feared that when he spoke he would do so in careful and toneless monosyllables.

'*Mary*,' he said hastily, crossing to kiss her. He felt, as he looked at her, a certain wrath and disappointment. She had a nebulous, unreal air, as of one who has permitted circumstance to define her visually – a nun, a prisoner, an actress . . . It was unlike Mary.

'You *look* well,' he said. She inclined her head. She had no idea of what she looked like, not having really seen herself in a mirror for months now, but she was fairly sure she didn't look well . . .

103

'Now come and see Seb and Ba and Kate,' instructed Mrs Marsh, ushering. 'And Evelyn,' she said. 'And then we'll have lunch at once.'

*　　*　　*

Mary and Sam sat where they were, the garden growing distant and dim as the snow fell with the darkness. There had been a moon last night – a bridal moon, veiled and ominous behind the running clouds – but now there were only snow flakes, hurrying down and gathering as mobs gather to overthrow tyrants.

Someone tapped at the window, pressed his face against the glass. Mary started and turned.

'Oh good lord,' she said. She called to her mother, raising her voice. 'It's the Chief Inspector. Can you open the back door to him?'

Sam stiffened.

Barbara in the midst of trying to appear to Hunter at once casual and irresistible, nearly died. 'Sam,' she whispered.

Mrs Marsh didn't notice. 'Drat the man,' she said. 'He keeps popping in to make sure we're all right and he *will* come through the hedge instead of round the front. He's a nosey old brute. What does he want now? Yes, Dennis?' she demanded rather brusquely, opening the kitchen door.

He was wearing his hat and overcoat and great big gum boots. She found it very difficult always not to stare at his feet.

He had come on a scanty pretext. The temperature was apparently dropping rapidly, heavy snow was forecast, the cars of Mrs Marsh's guests were out in the Close not wrapped up, and in some way the Chief Inspector seemed to feel himself responsible for all these eventualities.

'Well, there's nothing we can do about it,' said Mrs Marsh. 'We can hardly bring them in the house.'

'Blankets and waterproofs,' said the Chief Inspector. 'Cover them up.'

'Yes, yes,' said Mrs Marsh. 'I must go now. We haven't had lunch yet.' She wished she hadn't said that as it caused him to look rather shocked. 'You'll be in for a drink later?' she asked in her most ladylike voice. 'I did ask Vera.'

'Yes,' he agreed glumly. 'The wife did mention it. If the snow's not too bad,' he warned her.

'Since he retired, that man is so bored I believe his mind is going,' said Mrs Marsh, slamming the door. 'And what's more,' she added darkly, 'I don't see how he can possibly afford that house on a police pension.'

Barbara grew calmer. 'I thought the Walkers lived next door.'

'No, dear,' Mrs Marsh told her. 'She died and he sold up ages ago. I was sorry to see them leave.'

Sam glared through the window as the Chief Inspector stumped past. He disapproved of policemen and deplored the innate and shocking pessimism of a society which kept a police force. His own dealings with what he variously referred to as 'de fuzz', 'de filf' and 'de law' had not been pleasant. The police station where he had been taken on suspicion of being about to steal bicycles had been nasty with its smell of fear and vomit. A large framed photograph of a group of nineteenth-century policemen all wearing the morose, thoughtful expressions of a bunch of peelers who had signally failed to apprehend Jack the Ripper had brought to his face a rare grin which the officers present had chosen to interpret as saucy. The place had been like an unhealthy hive, with policemen buzzing in and out with their sad pollen of wrongdoers. (Traffic wardens, on the other hand, were more like wasps.) It had never actually crossed his mind that there was such a thing as an honest policeman.

Further out on the downs lived other retired policemen in flash bungalows, next-door to retired criminals, from whom they were indistinguishable in dress, tastes and overall attitude to the world. It was possible that Dennis was at least an honest policeman, since his house was modest by these standards and stood in Innstead, not out in the badlands of successful graft and – the rewards of sin – swimming pools. This, in itself, made him a lonely man. No one liked or trusted him. He had spent his life handling the dirty end of the stick and no one was grateful for it. He was as welcome in the homes of the righteous as a sewer rat, but seemed to feel no resentment – merely rather lost and deprived now that his retirement had rendered him purposeless. He did miss John. He had sent a wreath with an unsigned card – 'From a pal'. Mrs Marsh hadn't invited him to the funeral, but he had kept calling at the house until she had to ask if Vera would like to come to tea one day. They shared, to that extent, the same social code. Nevertheless, Mrs Marsh had never got over her feelings of unease and chilly dislike at finding a policeman, even a retired one, looming at her back door. She agreed with the neighbours that our policemen were wonderful, a splendid body of men, and had a very hard job to do, and so on, but no one in the Close had ever paused to consider where this wonderful body of men went to in the intervals of doing its hard job, and certainly no one had imagined it would emerge in the Close.

'I hope you're going to be polite to the Chief Inspector,' she said to Sam, feeling like someone about to introduce a dog to a cat. 'You don't have to talk to him. Just don't swear or . . .'

She stopped. She wanted to say 'Don't look at him' – since Sam's expression of sullen hostility was quite as offensive to the respectable middle-aged as rude words, but it sounded so odd.

'Just be good,' she said feebly.

Sam disliked and mistrusted the police on other grounds than merely social. Those of his fellow pupils who conformed he found odd enough – like waiters. In their obedience and subservience, they must, Sam felt, be joking. At any minute he expected them to throw off the cloak of humility, prod their masters with a jovial thumb and suggest that it was time the game was over. Soldiers, too, were incomprehensible. That anyone should submit himself, voluntarily or not, to a life of rules and regimentation was beyond his understanding, together with the whole concept of Queen and country. That this way of life also offered injury and death made it seem bizarrely perverse. But the police still struck Sam as the most peculiar. Burglars he understood perfectly, taking it as read that people who owned a great deal of money or property had come by it unjustly. History, as Sam saw it, proved the fact – as did the almost daily exposures of politicians and businessmen. Until held up to popular obloquy, the rich were universally respected because they were rich. Therefore, by aspiring to riches, the burglar was aspiring to respectability and it was hypocrisy to blame him for it. If what the rich possessed made them good, then it would make good anyone who possessed it. Sam could see no flaw in his argument and was shocked at the class treachery of working men who devoted their lives to halting or impeding this process of the redistribution of wealth and virtue. And, while the prisons were bulging with resentful burglars, there were several really determined and dedicated murderers, rapists, traitors, queers and spies running around in total freedom, sniggering conceitedly at the inefficacy of the detective force. The only imprisoned murderers were those accidental domestic ones, discovered on Monday morning drenched in blood, declaiming 'I never meant to do it and everything went black, m'lud'. For the most part, Sam knew, policemen owed their promotion to harrying black youths and arresting drunks, whom they rendered also incapable by kicking them in the crutch. And it was clear that when reluctantly compelled to investigate the activities of the upper classes the entire judicial system did its level best to ameliorate the consequences of those activities. As for his grandfather, the judge, and the like – where was the justice in permitting that class of persons most commonly stolen from to sit in judgment on that class of persons who most commonly stole? A certain bias seemed inevitable. Sam had no time for juries either. They were, by definition, already respectable and did as they were told.

'Pig,' said Sam aloud, and generally – of the Chief Inspector, his grandfather, his father, his headmaster and all others who sought to guide or contain him.

Now Barbara, in a flash of drunken enlightenment, recognised the similarity of her son to her sister and rose to blame someone for it.

'Mummy,' she said, pushing her mother towards the kitchen and closing the door.

'Lunch,' said Mrs Marsh, after a few difficult moments, with bar-deserving bravery.

She felt strong and capable. Barbara wasn't clever enough to be secretive and Mrs Marsh, who regarded secrecy as sinful, was glad. She could cope with honest hurt and recrimination, with the human and recognisable doubts of her younger daughter, but not with the sly, invidious resolutions of the elder. Mary was beyond help: it was insulting, denigrating – Mary's refusal of comfort and love. Barbara had damply confessed the discovery of her husband's infidelity, her son's intransigence, her own inadequacy – and for all these Mrs Marsh had the answer. Life must go on, she had told her, without considering the matter at all. It was plain that this was so. 'You must pick the raisins out of the cake,' she had said. 'Just look for what is good in your life.' Barbara, snivelling, had recognised the sense in this but had, to some extent, misunderstood her mother, confusing her advice with the prevalent wisdom which seemed to hold that sexual fulfilment, innocently pleasureable and free of guilt, was all that mattered. She slid on to the arm of the chair in which Hunter sat, endeavouring to lean as much of herself as was possible against as much of him as was available, while at the same time gazing across the room with an expression of tranquil reflection. The tension and urgency of her body, combined with what appeared to the onlooker to be a look of insane vacancy, was disturbing.

'Your glass is empty, dear,' said Evelyn nervously, reaching to the sideboard for a bottle – any bottle.

Barbara smiled brilliantly. 'Oh *thank* you,' she said, as though Evelyn had just ennobled her. 'Thank you so *much*.'

Into the silence that followed, Mrs Marsh announced that lunch must now be served. 'Mary,' she called peremptorily, 'come and sit down.'

*   *   *

Mary returned from Melys y Bwyd. The kitten's pale eyes were like rain-washed wood anemones, the tiny pads of its paws like blackberry pips and its claws like bramble thorns – the small, less serious ones high up the stem near the blossom . . . Robin on the whole had preferred the wild raspberries to the blackberries. One year they had spent the whole summer turning raspberries into jam. Robin had said it was *adorable*. No one else, as far as she knew, had ever described food as adorable. That was the year, she remembered meticulously, that Robin got covered in crows' egg, up a tree, poking down the nest with a clothes pole – not out of merry vandalism but in the eventual best interest of the crows, because they got down the chimney and it would be better for everyone if they were to leave. The careless structures of twigs in the chimney were a nuisance, causing damp grey yellow clouds of smoke to billow out when she first lit the fire, but it was worse to open up the silent cottage smelling of the wilderness, trapped, and see the sooty, perfect tracery of desperate wings on the white-washed walls and know that somewhere there lay a corpse to be disposed of. Crows were stupid enough to fall down chimneys but too stupid to get up them again. Silly birds, she thought, knowing that if it were daylight she could look across beyond the ridge and see the branches of the distant trees, clotted with crows' nests, but never Robin, never again, up or down a tree.

'What nonsense,' she said, freshly incredulous. 'You'd better take this cat,' she told her mother, handing it, now limply trustful, across her palm. 'It'll be better in the kitchen. Puss off.'

The ground at Melys y Bwyd would be icebound now, Robin's grave clasped iron-hard, Robin's bones as cold as stone. All around, the meadow grass would be silver-green and the mountain bracken red-gold; the trees plucked bare as dead birds save for the black yews and the fox umber of beech in the hedgerows. The hedgerows now, thought Mary with satisfaction, would be dry and pinched with frost – all gone their nuptial finery, the idle golden peace of summer days. Those hedgerows had much to answer for, decked for weddings, letting the hearse pass through them in the flowery dust. Once upon a time the lads of the village would have been looking to their staves now, plaiting a little cage, getting ready to beat the hedgerows in pursuit of the wren on the 26th. Such a sad, angry, godless day, the day after Christmas – the laughing, brutal young men carrying a dead caged bird high in triumph all round the boundaries to bury in the churchyard and allay misfortune for the coming year, and St Stephen stoned for feeding the poor. On Boxing Day the entire population would be pretty stoned – fat, sick, hungover and dreary with anti-climax and a surfeit of rich things.

* * *

'Comin', Mary?' enquired Mr Mauss. He was quite relaxed and clearly had no consciousness of being an intruder on this family scene. He had removed his beltless mac and his hat and wore a light-weight jacket and trousers, a striped shirt and strange feet-shaped shoes. He seemed to have aged since they last met and it didn't suit him. Like all his country-men, he was designed for youth, the ball-game, swimming the Atlantic. Now his handsome steak-and-milk-fed bones were obscured by drooping flesh, and his splendid teeth looked foolishly out of place between developing dewlaps.

Mary was thinking, 'The north wind doth blow and we shall have snow and what will the robin do then . . .'

'You do look well,' she said. She didn't habitu-ally greet other people with observations on their appearance – like a hunter sighting game and weigh-ing it up in his mind's eye.

'You look great,' said Mr Mauss, inexactly. He didn't much like Mary, who had once given it as her opinion that his great country was founded on heresy, genocide and greed – what the Americans themselves referred to as religious idealism, courage and enterprise. It was, he had considered, a quite uncalled-for remark.

Hunter whispered in Mary's ear as they paused in the hall. 'I'm sorry,' he said. 'I could have left him in London, but it didn't seem to occur to him that I would.'

'Well, of course you couldn't,' said Mary. Even she could see that. 'Christmas is sacred to them.'

Hunter giggled. They shared an image of the American Christmas – riches, reconciliations, tears, snow, success, sentiment, furs and firs, the shop windows shining like Heaven and everything good for sale.

'Jingle *bells*,' said Mary.

Mrs Marsh smiled, indulgently, if a little nervously. She had never understood their silly jokes but was glad to see Mary laughing. She wondered vaguely, not for the first time, why they had never married. They always got on so well.

She began to make people stand up so that she could pull their chairs to the tables. It was awkward and upsetting, and she wished momentarily that she could clap her hands and disperse everyone like the birds. So many people made a room even untidier than did present wrappings and string. Gamely, she coaxed and commanded. 'Evelyn, you sit here between Seb and Mr Mauss. Hunter, you get between Ba and Mary. Kate and Sam, you go and sit on the stairs . . .'

It was now that Mr Mauss revealed a hitherto unsuspected and wholly unwelcome aspect of his personality. He was *good with children* – he was fonder than Father Christmas of little children, fonder than Italian waiters, than politicians on polling day. Kate, he declared, should by no means sit outside on the stairs. She should sit on his knee if needs be. He didn't seem as fond of Sam.

Mrs Marsh could have crowned him with her tray. 'There isn't room,' she protested.

'Nahnsense,' said Mr Mauss roundly. At one point he even spoke of 'the little lady'.

114

Mrs Marsh gave in. She went so far against her principles as to put the sofa cushions on the floor for the children. Sam could hardly be banished alone to the stairs, though he was more than willing. She had never approved of Americans, ever since the days of G.I.s – funny-coloured uniforms and chewing gum . . .

'I'll serve in the kitchen,' she said flatly, not bothering to ask who would like what or how much of it.

'They'll have what they're given,' she muttered to Evelyn, who had maddeningly insisted on climbing over Mr Mauss to come out and help. The thought of waving vegetable dishes and boiling gravy boats above those close-crammed heads and her pretty chintz was altogether too daunting.

For once Sam wasn't hungry. He had eaten all the soft-centred chocolates from several of the boxes on the sideboard. He wished he hadn't. He liked the food he was given here. At Granny Lamb's now they would be sitting in the dining room with dogs dribbling at their sides. They'd be eating something like rotting pheasant with Smith's Crisps warmed up in the oven, and what his grandfather called 'bread poultice'; he ate it all the same, thought Sam – and the bitter walnuts from his own tree. Pauline, the housekeeper, wouldn't be there today; his grandmother would have to do the washing up. Though Pauline usually did all the kitchen work, he had never seen his grandmother actually touch her. It was as though the lower classes, no matter how

115

much they washed dishes or themselves, would never be clean enough for her to touch. (The pedigree dogs slept on her bed and licked her brown-spotted hands.)

Mr Mauss and Kate discussed poetry. Sam sat up at the mention of a poem by Tennyson called 'Marijuana in the Moated Grange' but lost interest when it turned out to be about a girl.

'That's the wise thrush,' trilled Kate, 'he sings each song twice over . . .'

Barbara's bit of turkey went down the wrong way.

Hunter beat her on the back and Evelyn brought her a glass of water.

'A lot of people die of choking these days,' Evelyn said conversationally. 'In American restaurants they keep a special thing for putting down people's throats. The average size of a piece of meat that people choke on is about like a cigarette packet. I expect Mr Mauss could tell you . . .'

First fine careless rapture, thought Barbara. Careless rapture . . . She hiccoughed violently and turned her face to Hunter's shoulder.

Oh help, thought Mrs Marsh.

'Hail to thee, blithe spirit,' waffled Kate.

Mary decisively clanged her knife down on the table.

Kate stopped speaking. She ate a potato slowly, one eye on her aunt. Despite her curiosity she had had enough sense not to question Mary on the effects of bereavement. She had considered offering the sweet sympathy of an innocent child, but had luckily thought better of that too. It would have been very foolish. Nevertheless her aunt's lack of interest made her nervous. She suspected, astonished, that of the two of them, Mary liked Sam the better – a preference unique in Kate's short experience.

'Bird thou never wert,' declaimed Mr Mauss.

Mrs Marsh saw worriedly that there still seemed to be a great deal of wine about. It reminded her indirectly of her mother, who had never approved of the Lord's actions at the marriage at Cana and was wont to suggest by way of excuse that he had probably turned the water into tonic wine, adding further that it must always be remembered that in those countries the water was undrinkable.

Hunter must have brought all these bottles, realised Mrs Marsh, and she hadn't thanked him.

Sebastian, his head inclined downwards, his face thoughtful, was shaking the peppermill – one of a pair, tall shiny wooden things, faintly phallic, a gift from the lady who owned the hairdressing salons. Mrs Marsh herself didn't much care for them – she preferred her dainty glass and silver cellar and pot – but at least she knew how to work them.

'You twist the top – Professor,' she said, permitting herself a moment's malice. 'Like this.' She leaned across and ground a liberal quantity of black pepper over Sebastian's sprouts.

Barbara was a little shocked that her mother should dare to tease Sebastian. 'He doesn't like too much,' she said.

Evelyn didn't think the party was going very well. She took her cracker and proffered an end to Hunter. 'Pull,' she invited.

The paper hat fell into his cranberry sauce, but Evelyn had the half with the joke. She unravelled it. 'What flies in the air and shaves?' she asked, announcing, as everyone seemed non-plussed, 'A hairy plane.'

'Oh, that was funny,' cried Mrs Marsh insincerely. 'Now, Kate, why did the bull rush?'

'Because it saw the cow slip,' responded Kate obediently.

Mr Mauss looked puzzled.

'What's the difference between a weasel and a stoat?' enquired Evelyn. No one knew. 'Well, a weasel is weasily distinguished and a stoat is stoatally different.'

Seb closed his eyes.

'Why did the lobster blush?' asked Evelyn, quickfire.

'Because it saw the salad dressing.' Kate was scornful.

'No,' said Evelyn triumphantly. 'Because it saw Queen Mary's bottom.'

Mrs Marsh remembered one of her mother's risky jokes – why is Queen Victoria like a flower pot? But it wasn't suitable for mixed company. Her mother had only told it as a concession – a treat for the girls when they were scouring pans or darning socks. Like the one about the Houses of Parliament passing motions in chambers. It was only

118

at Christmas that Mrs Marsh remembered things like that – her mother and the jokes, and the Band of Hope, and the mutton broth and sago pudding that were always Tuesday's dinner. She suddenly felt like Methuselah. She had passed through so many modes of everyday existence: from long to short to long to short skirts, from the copper and the dolly and the rubbing board to a geyser with constant hot water and now to a washing machine, from the old flat irons heating on the range to the neat little appliance that perched above her folded ironing board in the cupboard. The interminable nappies and linen sheets and shirts and tablecloths had been replaced by cotton wool and plastic and things that drip-dried. After the range she had had to get used to a gas stove, and now she had her clean electric oven. Soda and soft green soap had given way to plastic bottles of fat-fighting liquid. She was too sensible to feel regret, but she did feel extraordinarily old. And she wasn't old in present-day terms, she thought incredulously. Merely a senior citizen. I feel like God's granny, she thought, lost in the oddness of time.

'Whaddaya do if ya nose goes on strike?' asked Sam unexpectedly.

Only Kate knew the answer to this and she was, fortunately, not prepared to divulge it.

Barbara knew Sam too well to imagine it would be suitable for a family gathering, and her look threatened him with numerous deprivations if he proceeded.

Mrs Marsh rose hurriedly. 'Trifle or Christmas pudding?' she asked.

'I don't know that one either,' said Evelyn.

'I mean do you want to eat trifle or Christmas pudding?' said Mrs Marsh. Really, Evelyn could be dense at times.

'We'd better hurry,' she said. 'Dennis and Vera will be here soon.' She could kick herself for inviting them, but she *had* felt sorry for them, retired and alone and their boy – as they called him – away engineering somewhere in some unsafe country.

She dumped glass bowls in front of everyone, splashing a few spots of freshly melting brandy butter on Seb's cardigan. He dabbed at it, tutting, instead of ignoring it as a proper man would have done.

The sight of the kitchen horrified her. It looked as though a major accident had taken place rather than a Christmas luncheon. Evelyn hadn't scraped or separated the plates but had put them straight in the sink and filled it with water. Bits of turkey, grease and stuffing floated miserably about on top, interspersed with torn crackers. Part-filled bowls and glasses stood around on every surface, and the steam which was intended merely to heat the pudding had filled the room and escaped through the hall.

Into this chaos, if she knew him, would come the Chief Inspector and his wife. He seemed never to have heard of front doors. Probably used to bursting

120

in shoulder-first in the small hours, thought Mrs Marsh unjustly. She made sure the kitchen door was bolted. This once, she decided, he should do the thing properly.

'Barbara,' she implored, driven to appeal for help, 'clear the front room, and make the coffee.'

'I'll do it,' said Evelyn cheerfully.

'No,' said Mrs Marsh, louder than she had intended. 'You sit down and rest and talk to Mr Mauss.'

In the end Hunter did the tidying up. He did it beautifully and Mrs Marsh gazed at him with respect, wishing Sebastian were a bit more like him.

She put away the stilton and biscuits, which she hadn't offered to anyone. They would make too many crumbs and she was sure everyone had had enough to eat – except for Mary, who had messed about like a child, hiding her turkey under her potato and refusing parsnip and stuffing. She'd have to have an eggnog later, noted Mrs Marsh.

Evelyn was sitting on the sofa next to Sebastian, who was speaking of his work to Hunter. She looked bewildered. Seb's insistence on ordinary language and absolute clarity of expression rendered his discourse entirely unintelligible to the ordinary person.

Mrs Marsh felt warm affection for her. At one of Barbara's university parties Mrs Marsh had been lectured for half an hour by a small man, who looked to her as though he'd crawled up through a drain, on the importance of maintaining by breeding a standard of intelligence and physical beauty that was essential to civilisation. That much she had got of his drift. The points of the compass had come into it too – and there he had lost her.

Mr Mauss had also altered his demeanour and was speaking of important matters, but not, it seemed, to the satisfaction of Sebastian, who grew increasingly restive. At the words 'a person in an addictive situation' Seb lost patience. 'An addict,' he snarled. 'You mean an addict.'

'That is correct,' agreed Mr Mauss, imperturbably. Seb flung up his eyes behind his spectacles and exhaled loudly.

There were too many schools of thought here for Mrs Marsh to cope with. She herself liked the human comfort of the cliché.

'Well, life has to go on,' she said aloud, and went to wipe down the still warm oven. The kitchen was more or less back to normal, and she poured herself a medicinal tot of brandy. It was just possible, she reflected, that Dennis and Vera would think Sam's green hair was a party hat.

Evelyn was now describing the grief she had felt on learning that Venice was slowly sinking into the sea. Mr Mauss was agreeing that it was indeed a tragedy.

Mary, on the other hand, was rather pleased. She thought that she herself must have that instinct of tyrants, who, when bereaved or upset, respond by demanding huge destruction, comparable to the loss they feel that they themselves have suffered. 'Sod

Venice,' she thought idly, imagining the splash, plop, suck, as palaces, churches, paintings, statues, the horses of St Mark sank unprotesting into the turgid flood.

She retired to the back room and opened the window. Dry flakes of snow drifted in, as ready and accustomed as doves returning to their familiar cote. She left the window slightly ajar to feel the cold after the heat of the front room, and told herself that alive or dead she wouldn't undergo another Christmas. The year's accumulated ill-will seemed always to find expression at this time. Relations who throughout most of the year had the sense to stay apart confined themselves in small spaces to eat and drink too much. And not content with this they felt it necessary to invite people who were lonely because they were unpleasant or boring and no one liked them. They had to be made to participate since it was felt that no one should be alone on this of all days.

Alone – thought Mary. She put a shovelful of smokeless fuel on the fire, and it settled down obediently and burned. Like the hard black seeds her mother planted – they dropped unprotesting into the earth, grew, flowered and were cut, arranged by the W.I. and thrown away – all without a moment's query.

Mary was disobedient and perverse. 'No,' she said, sharply and aloud. It was, for Mary, quite a usual response. But answers abounded, and of them all death was the most neat and particular. There was no arguing with the imperial composure of the dead . . .

She drew a mahogany box from under her bed and began to burn the contents. Letters, birth and death certificates. Not many photographs since they had always made her uneasy – the pale faces and dark hair of dead wives, the polite expressions of doomed soldiers tricked out as for a party, the eager fearless smiles of past children beaming through old sunlight . . . She took out a child's drawings and letters, closed her eyes and put them back. There was no suitable repository anywhere in the world for such things. She thought perhaps she should eat them; for certainly, certainly when she went they would have to go with her.

'Do you want tea?' asked Hunter rather impatiently from the doorway. He'd forgotten the way suburban housewives had of stuffing guests from the city as though they'd travelled days and nights over deserts.

Mary turned her face to him and he looked away. 'Good heavens, no,' she said cheerfully.

Hunter relaxed. Firelight had a very odd quality, especially when it shone upwards on to a white face. For a moment he had feared that the humane thing to do would be to take the poker and put down the creature kneeling there in such pain.

'You are so right,' he said. The meals seemed to have run together. Lunch had drifted into tea time, and any minute now the people from next door would be in for drinks.

He helped Mary to her feet and she replaced her mahogany box and closed the window.

'We should really be off,' he said, not looking forward to Christmas night in London with Mr Mauss. 'Perhaps we should wait for the snow to ease up.'

'Oh, it's cold outside,' quoted Mary.

They hummed together a few bars of song, inflaming a new area of Barbara's endlessly receptive jealousy.

'You seem very cheerful,' she snapped at her sister, meaning 'Fraud, fake, hypocrite'.

'Oh, I am,' said Mary, grinning. Procne to mute Philomela grieving for her Itys, she thought. There was truly no song left in her.

Barbara had never been able to make out her sister. She found it impossible to know whether Mary knew something she didn't or was merely pretending, and it was hard to know which would have been the more infuriating. She smiled nervously at her grinning sister to let Hunter know that she and Mary understood one another.

They heard Mrs Marsh enunciating through the glass of the kitchen door: 'You'll have to go round the front. I don't want to let the cat out.'

Mary decided she couldn't face Dennis and Vera, and hurried back to her room.

Hunter wished he could go with her. He had, himself, a specific interest in policemen, but not in Chief Inspectors. It was the uniform, of course – not as glamorous as guardsmen or sailors, but an improvement on Spanish waiters in these hard and frugal times.

He opened the door. 'Crikey,' he said, impressed by the amount of snow that still fell.

'Brass-monkey weather,' said Dennis without emphasis or obscene intent, taking his coat off.

'It's warm in here,' said Vera, looking on the bright side.

'How's the cat?' asked the Chief Inspector, surprising Evelyn with this evidence of his uncanny detective abilities. She had kept the kitten secret.

'You were calling "Puss, puss",' he told her dropped jaw. His tone was stern but kind.

'It was my present to Mary,' said Evelyn guiltily. She hoped he wouldn't ask where she'd bought it, feeling sure that he would caution her and advise her that anything that was found should be handed in to the nearest police station.

'Dog man, myself,' he informed her, and she felt worse. She could see him with a great, grey, slavering, red-eyed alsatian striding the main street of Innstead – and the neighbours wouldn't let him have one.

'No dogs,' said Vera decisively, and Evelyn felt relieved. It was his wife who wouldn't let him.

No one, absolutely no one, was glad to see Dennis and Vera. Even Kate, who was usually pleased to meet a potential audience, could tell at a glance that they weren't poetic. The gregarious Mr Mauss could see that they weren't meaningful, and everyone else was a bit frightened of Dennis, except for Sebastian,

126

who probably thought he'd come to read the meter.

'You know everyone,' said Mrs Marsh. 'Have a drink.' She was exhausted and sick with drink. She longed to lie down, but she was responsible for all these people. 'Sherry, whisky?' she asked. She simply couldn't be bothered to introduce anyone. They all knew their own names, dammit, she thought, with a restoring rush of temper, as they stood around, silent.

Hunter poured two glasses of sherry and handed them to the newcomers. He began to talk.

Mrs Marsh sat down, thankful for Hunter. He reminded her of her mother, who could calmly wipe obscuring tides of blood from a wound and pronounce it not mortal, while everyone else had fainted; who could come into a house in the small hours of emergency and, without removing her hat, restore order. She was *reliable*, thought Mrs Marsh, and Hunter was too; whereas Sebastian – she glanced at him with the venom of any music-hall mother-in-law – responded to difficulty with angry criticism, or sulking silence. Very helpful, she thought bitterly. For a moment she felt, like Mary, that death was blind or malevolent to take the beloved and leave the Sebastians. She was too tired and cross to regret these uncharitable Christmas-Day reflections. Life was unfair, and that's all there was to it. She felt pity for Mary like sudden spring rain, but it brought her no relief. She shivered in the hot little room. It would always be the Robins who were at risk – young and so wild and foolish. *Too* young to leave their mothers, she thought sadly. The Sebastians were hardly at risk at all except for overeating and the danger of summer lightning.

'I'm writing a book of verse,' said Kate, brazenly, to Hunter. She had been waiting for a suitable opportunity to point this out, but none had so far offered itself.

Hunter wanted to reply 'Then stop it at once', but instead remarked that that was nice.

Mrs Marsh brightened. 'Show Hunter, darling,' she said.

'*What* a clever girl,' said Vera disapprovingly.

Hunter could have screamed. He couldn't remember when he'd last met someone who wasn't writing a book.

Kate waited, a slow expression of hurt spreading over her normally bland countenance as Hunter was silent.

'You must let me read it,' he said at last resignedly, beckoning up the responsive platitudes. In the world of books it was never worth saying what you meant. Extreme caution was necessary in negotiating your way through the sensibilities of people who wrote, and while this child already clearly had an ego like the liver of a Strasbourg goose it offered her no protection against rejection. Quite the contrary.

Hunter read a poem under the eager intent gaze of Kate and Mrs Marsh.

'Very good,' he said flatly, closing the book and handing it back. 'Very good indeed for her age,' he added as they both obviously found this praise inadequate.

Kate reopened the book and handed it back to him. 'Have you read that one?' she asked.

Hunter read it. 'It's very . . .' he began. 'Excellent,' he ended heartily.

It was Barbara who saved him, for once putting her own needs before those of her child. Ever since the temperature had begun to drop so noticeably she had been worrying about whether she had remembered to turn off the water at the mains, and if not whether Seb had remembered to leave his key with the archaeologist up the road who was staying at home for the holidays and had promised to keep an eye on things. She wasn't sure that this man would be any more useful than Seb in an emergency, but at least he could go and have a look. None of this did she dare confide to her husband, who would be very angry, and would blame her personally for the ice and snow.

She ousted Kate and sat down by Hunter. 'Don't be a nuisance,' she told the baffled child. 'Hunter doesn't want to talk business today.'

Kate took her poems straight to Mr Mauss. An initial American publication was not something she had planned, but she could think of nothing against it.

Barbara closed her eyes and put her head back, breathing in the scent of Hunter – a faintly woolly, bachelor smell, quite unlike the smell of a husband. He smelled of his little house, comforting, secure. Now the thought of her probably ruined home no longer troubled her – icicles in the airing cupboard, the staircase a glacier. She took a sip of wine and snapped her fingers – pooh. She thought of Hunter's house instead. She had been there twice – no, three times: always on a Sunday afternoon and always because Seb needed to see Hunter. They had taken the children and had tea. It was odd to remember that she hadn't much enjoyed it at the time, worrying about the drive home in the dark, and getting the children's school things ready for the next day . . . It had had that damp, sweet, oddly womanless smell, and she had teased him a little – about the dishes in the sink, the mouse tracks in the pantry, the stew left in a cupboard from one week to the next. There had been lamplight too, and firelight and a lavender bush outside the front door, and bees in hives in a field, and little brown birds. Once she had rested on Hunter's hard bed when she had a migraine. She had thought nothing of it at the time, she remembered, amazed at her ingratitude and yet proud that she had been so untouched by the wonder of lying on Hunter's bed. She hadn't even looked around for evidence of women. It seemed never to change, Hunter's house. Each time it was the same: the same books, the same cups, the same comb in the bathroom. Perhaps in the New Year Seb would ask her to take his MS. down to Hunter. She would leave the children with her friend Ruth and a cold supper for Seb and arrive early, before Hunter got home. The door was warped and stuck on the flagstones when you pushed it open. She could see herself pushing it, feel her spirits sink as she thought it was locked, pushing again, harder. It opened. She was inside, she was lighting the oil lamps – she had no idea how to go about this, but inspiration would come to her. She lit the fire. The little house was growing warm and glowing with pearly light. Hunter had left steak – no, chops. She would make a hotpot and the homely smell would welcome him. He would be so surprised to see the lights gleaming through the snow, and smell lamb. It didn't occur to her that anyone approaching home under these unexpected conditions might turn straight round and come back with a policeman. Potatoes? Onions? She frowned in the effort to remember where they were kept. The silly boy would have left them too long and they'd be sprouting. But she would have done her shopping on the way. She would have bought fresh vegetables for Seb. Hunter should have them. She would lay the table, but Hunter didn't seem to have any table-cloths and the table top wasn't very nice. There was a paisley counterpane in one of the bedrooms – she'd use that. She checked that there was wine in the cupboard by the fire. She made the bed when she took the counterpane – she wished she had a pink frilled nightgown like a rose to lay on the pillow beside Hunter's pyjamas. She wished she could happen to have about her clean white sheets, smelling of gardens. Then she remembered that Hunter's sheets smelled only of Hunter, and she shivered with wholly unaccustomed libidinous delight.

'Barbara . . .' he was saying, and she was back in Innstead – the lamps in Hunter's house still glowing, the hotpot simmering. But the blizzard was raging here – not forcing her to stay alone with Hunter, but keeping Hunter here with Mr Mauss and Evelyn and Dennis and Vera and Seb and the children and so on, as though a fairy had given her a wish and she had got it wrong, forgetting to specify that she wished to be snowed in *alone* with Hunter. And even Hunter's actual presence was somehow less convincing than her imaginings. She was a little disappointed in him.

'I thought you were going to drop your glass,' said Hunter, who was feeling squashed between Barbara and Vera.

'I like the painting,' said Vera, looking at the framed representation of the lunatic asylum on the mantelpiece.

'Do you?' said Mrs Marsh, surprised.

Evelyn waited.

'Evelyn did it,' said Mrs Marsh hastily. 'She's very clever.'

'We knew you painted,' said Vera. 'Dennis has seen you with your easel and that.'

'I haven't been doing it long,' said Evelyn. 'I'm still learning, really.'

'I've been writing poetry for years,' said Kate, crudely.

She and Evelyn glared at each other, competing for the uncertain and wavering limelight.

'I admire people who do things,' said Vera. 'Dennis did pottery once, but he didn't stick to it.'

'I've got a lot more at home,' said Evelyn. 'You can come and see them if you like.'

132

'Now,' said Barbara suddenly. 'She's very good,' she added explanatorily. 'You should really see her things.'

Evelyn was gratified but puzzled. She didn't think Barbara had ever seen her paintings. 'When . . . ?' she began.

'Sam,' said Barbara, 'wipe the window and see what the weather's doing.'

'No'gorracloff,' said Sam.

'Well, use your hand.' Barbara was impatient.

'I'm no'gonna use my *han*',' said Sam indignantly. 'Tha's all uvver peopew's condense' breff.'

No one would have suspected him of such fastidiousness.

'Well, get a tissue from the kitchen and use that,' suggested his mother.

'Can' fin' one,' came Sam's voice.

Barbara almost despaired. Sam seemed to have inherited all his father's impracticability without even his intellect. Surely most normal people would have ascertained by now whether it was snowing or not. 'Open the door and look,' she said, in a brave effort to resolve this apparently insoluble problem.

'No, don't do that,' said Mrs Marsh. 'You'll let all the cold in.'

'If you turned the wireless on you might get the weather forecast,' observed Evelyn.

'Dennis,' asked Vera with simple faith, 'is it still snowing?'

Now Mr Mauss rose from the hearth where he was playing snakes and ladders with Kate. Resolutely he wiped the window pane with his clean white handkerchief. 'It's snowing fit to bust,' he told them.

Thwarted, Barbara poured herself another drink. Paradoxically her faint disillusion with Hunter had given her the courage and determination to get him alone, all to herself. He seemed rather more available. 'No,' she would have said, detaining him as they all left for the feast of art at Evelyn's. 'Not you, Hunter. I want to ask you something.' It would have to be something about Mary, she had decided unscrupulously, killing two birds with one stone. Her question would be personal, faintly psychiatric, the kind that only he as an old friend could answer, and that would necessarily exclude Mary's presence. It hadn't yet occurred to her to doubt that when they were alone Hunter would, in some fashion, declare himself.

'Hunter,' said Mrs Marsh, knowing now upon whom she could rely in this gathering, 'would you ask Mary if she'd like a hot drink?'

Hunter rose gladly and Barbara got up to pour herself another drink, not hot, she thought, but very strong.

After a while Mrs Marsh followed Hunter to discover the answer to her question. He sat opposite Mary, laughing.

'No, she wouldn't,' he said, remembering, as Mrs Marsh opened the door.

Mrs Marsh felt let down. 'I wish you'd come through, Mary,' she said. 'It seems awfully rude to

Dennis and Vera you sitting in here. As though you were avoiding them.'

'If I were a man,' said Mary broodingly, 'I think I'd rather be called dogshit than Dennis.'

'Oh, well if you're in that mood,' said Mrs Marsh, 'you'd better stay in here. Come on, Hunter, leave Misery on her own.'

'Besides,' Mary said, 'Vera's face looks like a tumour.'

Mrs Marsh was furious with Mary for saying something so unkind and disgusting. Nevertheless she inhaled her next sip of sherry instead of swallowing it as she had intended. It went up her nose and started coming out of her eyes, as she wondered what would happen if her nerves impelled her to ask Vera whether she would like to come upstairs and powder her tumour. Her face *was* unhealthily bright and shiny. Mrs Marsh spluttered and dashed her eyelids with the top of her finger.

'What are you laughing at?' asked Evelyn. 'Share the joke.'

'I'm not laughing,' said Mrs Marsh, furious with herself.

'Well, here's one,' said Evelyn, reading from a strip of paper. 'What did the god say when his thunderbolt boomeranged?'

'God knows,' said Mrs Marsh, uncaring.

'I'm Thor,' revealed Evelyn.

Only Sam immediately saw the point of this and he didn't think it was funny.

Restlessly, Barbara got up. Her vision was clear

but restricted. She tripped over a footstool but made unerringly for the door, the hall and the door beyond, where she saw Hunter as though isolated in a circle and Mary a threatening blur on the periphery.

'I just wish everyone would stay in one place for five minutes,' said Mrs Marsh. 'It's like a pantomime – Mary's in and out like a fiddler's elbow and now Barbara's doing it too.' Normally she wouldn't have spoken so disloyally, but it seemed that this Christmas Day it wasn't the Prince of Peace but the Lord of Misrule who held sway, and Mrs Marsh didn't care for anarchy.

'Do come through, Hunter,' said Barbara.

She leaned backwards and held out both hands to him where he lay on the floor. It was a totally unnatural gesture and one that it was impossible to respond to gracefully.

He got up hurriedly and touched one of her out-stretched hands. 'Come on, Mary,' he said.

'You've been rejec'-neject-neglecting us, Hunter,' said Barbara, seizing the tail of his coat.

Mary sat down by Sebastian, reflecting that one of the consolations of death was that when it came very close it at least inhibited the invincibly rational from making their usual attempts to disabuse the credulous of their belief in God and the after-life. Even Seb, it seemed, had sufficient delicacy not to speak when there was plainly nothing he could say to her. He was none the less, she considered, a pretty terrible man. He had no garden round his mind.

Dennis looked thoroughly uneasy. He had, of

136

course, been told that Seb's father was *the* Mr Justice
Lamb and had been speaking to Seb with a curdling
mixture of brusque bonhomie and deference. Twice
he had referred to 'this moment in time', twice he
had called Seb 'Sir' and once he had called him
'Seb'.

Sebastian, as was his way, had simply ignored
him; and now the Chief Inspector sat on the edge
of his chair, his elbows on his parted knees, twirling
his glass in his fingers, while drops of sweat emerged
on his temples and under his eyes.

Vera was less nervous. Evelyn was talking to her,
and sometimes Vera said 'Ooh, lovely'.

Soon they would go, thought Mary. Christmas was
like a storm washing people to and fro to end up,
unwanted, in each other's homes: Kate lying like
flotsam on the rug, the extraordinarily alien American, the policeman hopelessly out of place, Sebastian
bored almost insensible and Barbara lost in unhappy
fantasy. What was needed was an ebb tide.

Sam, with youthful charity, actually felt sorry for
the Chief Inspector. He didn't himself often suffer
from social unease but he knew it when he saw it
from his experience with his father's undergraduates.
While it was true that the Chief Inspector would
probably be happier kicking some miscreant to death,
it was still unfair to expect him to sit around in a
little room talking to a clever, unresponsive man
whose dad could probably have had him thrown out
of the Force if he'd wanted to.

Sam raised his eyebrows at Dennis, meaning to

indicate 'You don't have to be polite. That's only my father.'

'Well, young man,' said the Chief Inspector, feeling more on his own ground with this naughty-looking youth.

Sam lowered his eyebrows. The Chief Inspector was incorrigible. His next words would probably be 'We've been watching you for some time'.

'Pig,' muttered Sam again, not quite quietly enough.

'Well, here's to God,' said Mary, creating a diversion and pouring herself a whisky.

They stared at her, uncomprehendingly.

'It's his birthday,' she said.

Nearly everyone was shocked.

Mrs Marsh felt a great desire to bang together the heads of her daughter and grandson. Christmas was bad enough without this sort of behaviour.

'I didn't notice you going to midnight Mass,' she said very crossly indeed. As a rule, she avoided all mention of Catholicism in public, considering it, even after her years of marriage to her dear John, not quite nice.

'I didn't go,' explained Mary.

'The Queen, God bless her,' toasted the Chief Inspector, seeing a raised glass and entering into the spirit of the thing. He felt much more at ease with a little formality: uniforms, gruff laughter and someone requesting that everyone should be upstanding.

'Bless her,' echoed Vera and Evelyn, hastily putting to their lips their empty glasses.

There was nothing else for it. Mrs Marsh poured everyone another drink.

'She looked lovely on telly,' said Vera, moist-eyed.

Sam stared at them in mingled disgust and disbelief.

Mary sat down. Christ had no time for royalty. King Herod was, to him, not His Gracious Majesty, but – 'that fox'. Today the little animals were in the shade, and the monarch to the fore, the madness of the English again evident but concentrated on their other obsession. This dimension of madness took the form of a grateful tenderness towards the unimaginably rich and privileged; a tearfully joyous, knee-sore loyalty to the witless descendants of ruthless, incompetent, raging tyrants and murderers. Not since the Monk Guitand had anyone declined a favour from the hand of the monarch. This monk had hot-footed it home to Normandy, refusing the bishopric which the Conqueror would have thrust upon him, declaring that when he thought of the crimes by which England had been won, he 'trembled to touch it, with all its wealth, as though it glowed with the fires of hell'.

'What did Harold say at the Battle of Hastings?' she asked, still lost in the mists of time but not of a mind to reveal her true thoughts.

' "'old on 'arf a mo' ",' said Sam. ' "I've got somefin' in me eye." '

'Correct,' said Mary.

Grinning death was the king of the world and the preferment he offered was a too great change of status, transformation. His favouritism was feared beyond all else and his touch shunned.

Mary mistrusted monarchs, but most of all King Death who had left his great halls and, in a horrid parody of democracy, walked among his subjects choosing randomly whom he should elevate.

'You shouldn't be drinking,' said Mrs Marsh. 'What did the doctor say?' She was fed up with all the silly jokes. 'I think we should go now and look at Evelyn's pictures. Hunter and Mr Mauss will have to leave soon.'

'Snow's bad,' said the Chief Inspector.

'Yeah,' agreed Mr Mauss, looking through his porthole of condensation-free window. 'It's the sort the Lapps call *pjff*. You can't drive in it.'

'What do you mean?' demanded Mrs Marsh, thrusting him aside and peering out. 'You're probably used to American snow – Chicago, the Rockies. This is English snow. Yours is probably more like Swiss snow.'

'My grandmother on my mother's side was Swedish,' said Mr Mauss. 'And I know snow!'

You don't know *English* snow, thought Mrs Marsh wildly, refusing to contemplate the possibility that Hunter and his American might have to stay the night.

'Be great for the kids in the morning,' said Mr Mauss complacently. He nudged Kate, who lay gracelessly sprawled on the hearthrug in a mess of snakes and ladders, with an affectionate foot. 'Build a snowman, huh?' he said.

'It's probably only local,' said Mrs Marsh. 'It'll be clear on the main roads.'

The Chief Inspector and Mr Mauss both shook their heads with stolid certainty.

Evelyn, seeing Mrs Marsh's expression, was reminded of a lady lunatic at the asylum who went about all day, poor soul, crying in the most piteous, gentle and beseeching way 'No more. Oh, no more' – as though one further straw would be that final straw which would break her sad heart before she remembered to put it in her hair. It was so unlike Mrs Marsh's usual expression that Evelyn was quite alarmed. 'What is it, dear?' she asked, following Mrs Marsh out of the room.

'These people put years on me,' said Mrs Marsh exhaustedly, sitting down at the kitchen table. 'I think they're going to have to stay the night – and it's only a bit of snow.'

'Not Dennis and Vera,' said Evelyn, astonished.

'No, of *course* not Dennis and Vera. They've only got to crawl through the hedge. Hunter, and that – American.' Mrs Marsh was feeling acutely xenophobic and regretted the impulse which had led her to invite Dennis and Vera and agree to offer hospitality to Mr Mauss. She had a haunted, crepuscular sensation as of some encroaching disease or disaster. Influenza or a family crisis were imminent and strangers would undoubtedly get in the way.

'Is it too tiring for Mary?' asked Evelyn. 'I know she doesn't like seeing a lot of people. I suppose in the circumstances . . .'

141

'What circumstances?' asked Mrs Marsh wearily. 'I don't believe she's as ill as she'd like to be. I don't believe she's going to die. She just wants to. She's wicked,' concluded Mrs Marsh in shame.

'Cheer up,' said Evelyn uneasily. 'I thought she seemed bright enough today.'

'Well, if she was, it's because she doesn't care,' said Mrs Marsh obscurely.

'Eh?' said Evelyn, squinting.

'Oh, I don't know,' said Mrs Marsh. 'There were some men in the war like that. John said they'd get these letters from home and then they wouldn't care.'

'Care?' asked Evelyn, hopelessly puzzled.

'They'd get these letters saying their wife had left them or got bombed or something, and then they wouldn't care *what* happened – if they got shot or not or anything. They were suddenly brave, only it wasn't really brave . . .'

'Oh,' said Evelyn in a false tone of enlightenment.

'Never mind,' said Mrs Marsh, pulling herself together. She'd said too much already. 'We'd better get back to the others.'

'You should stop frowning like that,' Evelyn told her. 'You'll get terrible wrinkles.'

'I've *got* wrinkles,' said Mrs Marsh. 'And no wonder.'

'I'll take everyone to see my pictures,' said Evelyn. 'We'll get a better idea of the weather if we go out in it. Come along, all,' she cried, doing a brief, but spirited and bracing gallop into the hall. 'Coats, hats. We're going to my house.'

142

'I'll stay here and tidy up,' said Mrs Marsh.

'No, you won't,' said Evelyn. 'You need a breather and I'll make you all a nice hot cup of coffee.'

She was surprised to find that the two meekest members of the party were adamant in their refusal to join her. Barbara, sitting alone on the sofa and clutching a glass in one hand and a bottle of sherry in the other, so tightly that her knuckles shone, said that she had a headache, and didn't, anyway, really know much about painting. Music – here her voice faltered – was her preference. Hunter, having declined politely, had, Evelyn suspected, locked himself in the bathroom since she couldn't see him anywhere; but she could hardly follow him up and rattle the door handle. There was no point, of course, in asking Sam or Mary.

'Come on,' she urged as everyone struggled into their coats. 'Be careful not to let kitty out. Oh, we should sing carols,' she cried, as they trudged rather bitterly across the Close.

*   *   *

Evelyn's house smelt quite different from Mrs Marsh's – faintly of past meals, rather than of meals in preparation, which was the only cooking smell which Mrs Marsh would permit. She had cold, glaring central ceiling lights, where Mrs Marsh had shaded table lamps, and her sitting room had only a square of carpet in the middle of the floor. The alligator (it was a mugger, Evelyn told them, on account of how its teeth were disposed) hung above the fireplace, flanked by two of Evelyn's pictures. It gave the room an oddly propitiatory, explanatory air as though Evelyn were appealing: 'I don't cook or keep house very well, but you see I am a lovable *eccentric* and here is the proof.'

It didn't cut any ice with Vera. 'What a horrible thing,' she said. 'I don't know how you can bear to look it in the eye. It'd give me the willies.'

'I like it,' said Evelyn huffily. 'I call him Claud.'

Sebastian made one of his noises, expressive, probably, of limitless contempt, but Kate found herself envying Evelyn this reptile. 'I think it's silly,' she said jealously. 'My friend Jessica's got a stuffed fox. Called Augustus,' she added.

'I'm gonna buy you a bear,' said Mr Mauss, pinching Kate's ear.

'Ooooh,' gurgled Kate, 'a weal one?'

'A-great-big-bear,' vowed Mr Mauss, hugging her. They swayed together from foot to foot, repeating this phrase and giggling.

'Well!' said Evelyn loudly. 'I've got pictures all over the house. Where would you like to start?'

'Let's start with coffee,' said Mrs Marsh, sitting down at a square oak table, on a chair made of oak and artificial leather. She unbuttoned her coat and stretched her legs out. She hoped Mr Mauss wasn't a paedophile.

'Evelyn,' she said boldly, 'could you put up Hunter and Mr Mauss if the snow doesn't stop?'

'Yes, of course,' said Evelyn obligingly, 'if they don't mind sharing a room.'

144

Mr Mauss seemed to take this offer for granted too. 'That's OK,' he said, continuing to rock back and forth with Kate.

It occurred to Mrs Marsh that they were both slightly drunk. 'I'll help you with the coffee,' she said to Evelyn. 'It'll sober – warm us – up.'

'Are you cold?' asked Evelyn surprised. 'I'll turn on the log. I don't really feel the cold – I think it's because I'm so used to painting on the downs in all weathers.' She emphasised the word 'painting' very slightly.

'I like this one,' said Dennis, closely inspecting a muddy study of some distant trees hanging to the left of Claud.

'I did that in April,' said Evelyn, putting out cups and saucers and teaspoons – rejecting one or two spoons after a closer look and putting them back in the drawer.

Those would be the eggy ones, thought Mrs Marsh. She resigned herself to a time of undrinkable coffee and art.

*   *   *

'Meanwhile the Protestants . . .' said Mary. 'What do you want to do, Hunter? Can't you really drive in this?'

'No,' said Hunter.

Barbara, posed on the arm of the sofa in the front room, shifted slightly. She had cleaned her teeth and put on fresh lipstick, but still felt unreal, blinkered and a little deaf. Knowing that Hunter had stayed behind, she was awaiting his declaration.

After a while when he still hadn't appeared she stood up. A mistake. She took a sip of brandy from the decanter to steady her head.

'Hunter,' she called. '*Hunter*.'

Hunter glanced at Mary, faintly alarmed. 'She's awfully *drunk*,' he said.

'You'd better go and see what she wants,' said Mary.

He went into the front room and looked around. 'Here,' said someone, half whispering.

He went back into the hall and looked round there. Barbara was half way up the stairs, beckoning. Puzzled, he went towards her and she sped upwards to the tiny landing.

Like a fool, he followed her.

'Kiss me,' she demanded as he drew level. She seized his lapel and breathed into his mouth.

'Ugh,' said Hunter, recoiling. She clutched him tighter and they struggled slightly on the tiny dais. Her foot slipped from the top step.

'You must kiss me or kill me,' she told him, gripping him now with both hands.

'I will do neither of those things,' said Hunter exasperatedly, trying to free himself.

Abruptly Barbara let go and slid downstairs. Unhurt but quite crushed, she sat at the foot of the stairs, her legs splayed out like a dutch doll's, and wept.

Sam, who was frying himself a plateful of eggs, emerged backwards from the kitchen to see what all the fuss was about. He was shocked to find his mother lying drunk on the floor, with that pooftah standing over her, looking annoyed. He went back to the stove and slipped his eggs on to two pieces of toast. Tears of embarrassment and rage and childishness made it difficult for him to locate the tomato sauce. He didn't really feel hungry now but ate his eggs sitting at the kitchen table. He could just about get a whole egg into his mouth.

'Mary,' said Hunter plaintively, 'what shall we do with Barbara?' His neatness, his domestic efficiency wouldn't stretch to coping with drunken and lecherous women.

'She ought to sleep it off,' suggested Mary. 'She doesn't usually do this, so black coffee would make her sick.'

'Well, I'm not taking her to bed,' said Hunter, wishing simultaneously that he had put that differently and waiting for Mary to frame some witticism.

But Mary couldn't be bothered. 'I'll put a blanket over her,' she said. 'With any luck she'll come round before they get back.'

She got Aunt Gwennie's dark, soft tartan rug from her room and approached her sister.

Barbara began to scream. The kitten in the kitchen by the warm stove started up, terrified, fur erect – perhaps thinking itself back on the black cold downs, small and open to the strange perverted predators of town-bordering heath.

Sam sat quite still, gazing steadfastly at the tomato ketchup.

'Bloody hell,' said Mary, stepping back and clutching the rug.

Barbara's eyes hung low and red in her face. Her head was thrust forward, her skirt was rucked up and now she was speaking with unprecedented fluency. She spoke of jealousy and anger and love and loss and infinite perfidy.

Mary stared at her. Having forgotten that anything but death mattered at all, she was bewildered by her sister's anguish.

Sam could bear it no longer. Seizing a jug from the draining board he filled it with water and loping the short distance from the sink to the stairs flung it over his mother.

'You might have rinsed it out first,' said Hunter, feeling again the onset of hysteria. Coffee grounds trickled down Barbara's forehead and reposed above her collar bone.

*   *   *

It was to this scene that the others returned.

They saw Barbara lying on the floor, wet and dirt-streaked and weeping, Mary poised over her with a rug as though her sister was a budgerigar who would not be silent for the night, Hunter giggling feebly and Sam, his face white, clutching an empty jug.

'What mischief is this?' enquired Sebastian, smacking his son's head.

Barbara struggled to her knees, a primitive

mother-instinct bared by drink. 'Don't you touch
. . .' she began, falling back against the newel post.

Sam made for the door, pausing only to thrust his
jug upon Mr Mauss. Kate flung herself after him
into the night, crying in ringing thespian tones,
'Sam, oh Sam, don't *do* this!'

'Will someone shut that child up,' said Hunter,
regaining his calm and slamming the door, nearly
catching Kate's nose as he hauled her in.

'Ow,' she said.

'I'll go after him,' said the Chief Inspector.

'No,' said Barbara very loudly. 'You leave him
alone.' She looked hot-eyed at Sebastian. '*You* go,'
she said to her husband. '*You* go and get him.'

Sebastian was a small man but his violence darkened the hall, his cream pale face set in carven,
godlike lines of anger and disgust. He was immovable, and Barbara understood that she could fall
right over the edge of despair into death and he
would still be immovable because he was an entirely
reasonable man.

She went, herself, into the Close.

'Sam,' she shrieked.

Hunter followed her.

'Pig,' she shouted at him.

The squirrel in his drey awoke and peered down,
astonished, a querying paw curled against his
breast. The quarrelsome birds, peaceful in the darkness, shifted in their puffed and staring feathers.
The teddy bears in all the little houses clapped their
cloth paws over their cloth ears.

149

What will the neighbours think, wondered Mrs Marsh, statutorily, past caring. She, alone, had sufficient courage to approach the distraught, coffee-scented woman and draw her home.

Vera stood by the door clutching her bag with both hands and looking eminently useless and unhelpful. Dennis, too, was at a loss, like a person stripped of authority in the presence of strange, but not criminal, behaviour – as indeed he was. His natural human responses had atrophied years ago under the pressure of applied order.

'Deary me,' said Evelyn, 'what a to-do.' She pressed Vera's coat upon her. Evelyn's father having been a bank manager, she was qualified in such extreme circumstances to give orders to a mere policeman's wife. 'Run along home,' she said, adding, 'Off you go, Dennis. Vera looks tired.'

Mr Mauss was uncomfortable and rather angry. The corner of his mouth twitched a little. His easy manners, his familiarity with the workings of the human mind as disclosed by psychiatry, his overall goodwill were inadequate to deal with this nasty scene, and he had no desire at all to witness the drunken discomfiture of an English lady. It upset his ideals. Besides, he was American and liked all events and occasions – no matter how unfortunate or bloody – to end in sweetness and reconciliation, and it seemed most unlikely that these people would finish the evening in each others' arms singing.

'Come along,' said Evelyn. 'You two can spend the night at my house.' They could all have some more coffee, sitting round the table. It would be like the days when her brothers were young, sitting up late into the night, planning a hiking trip. 'If we're quick,' she promised, 'we'll just catch the news and the main points of the Queen's speech.'

'I hope you feel better, dear,' she said to Barbara. 'Come across in the morning and have a cup of coffee.' She had thought it was Mary who was the drinker and wondered for a moment, as Mrs Marsh had feared she might, how these girls had been brought up. Bad blood, she thought, and put the thought aside.

All Barbara would feel like in the morning, thought Hunter, would be a stiff formaldehyde. It seemed unlikely that he would see much even of Mary after this.

'Goodbye,' he said regretfully.

*   *   *

Mary had gone back to her room. She opened the French windows and went out into the garden.

She could see the snow falling through the small rounded light from the downstairs lavatory window, a light as pure as from any cathedral clerestory. It fell with such soft determination in the still silence – soundless, weightless: gentle alien blossom that would melt, if she waited long enough, into familiar wetness, tears on the face: bathetic melting, mud in the garden, slush on the roads, useless tears.

She lifted her face to the angelic descent in the

muted darkness, to the movement compelled by something other than desire, the lifeless idle movement of the drowned, to the veil, grave cloths, the floating sinking cerements, untroubled by blood, by colour: the discrete, undeniable, intractable softness of the slow snow in the night and the silence . . .

'Robin . . . ?' she said.

MORE ABOUT PENGUINS, PELICANS, PEREGRINES AND PUFFINS

For further information about books available from Penguins please write to Dept EP, Penguin Books Ltd, Harmondsworth, Middlesex UB7 0DA.

In the U.S.A.: For a complete list of books available from Penguins in the United States write to Dept DG, Penguin Books, 299 Murray Hill Parkway, East Rutherford, New Jersey 07073.

In Canada: For a complete list of books available from Penguins in Canada write to Penguin Books Canada Limited, 2801 John Street, Markham, Ontario L3R 1B4.

In Australia: For a complete list of books available from Penguins in Australia write to the Marketing Department, Penguin Books Australia Ltd, P.O. Box 257, Ringwood, Victoria 3134.

In New Zealand: For a complete list of books available from Penguins in New Zealand write to the Marketing Department, Penguin Books (N.Z.) Ltd, Private Bag, Takapuna, Auckland 9.

In India: For a complete list of books available from Penguins in India write to Penguin Overseas Ltd, 706 Eros Apartments, 56 Nehru Place, New Delhi 110019.

A CHOICE OF PENGUINS

☐ *Further Chronicles of Fairacre* **'Miss Read'**

Full of humour, warmth and charm, these four novels – *Miss Clare Remembers, Over the Gate, The Fairacre Festival* and *Emily Davis* – make up an unforgettable picture of English village life.

☐ *Callanish* **William Horwood**

From the acclaimed author of *Duncton Wood*, this is the haunting story of Creggan, the captured golden eagle, and his struggle to be free.

☐ *Act of Darkness* **Francis King**

Anglo-India in the 1930s, where a peculiarly vicious murder triggers 'A terrific mystery story . . . a darkly luminous parable about innocence and evil' – *The New York Times*. 'Brilliantly successful' – *Daily Mail*. 'Unputdownable' – *Standard*

☐ *Death in Cyprus* **M. M. Kaye**

Holidaying on Aphrodite's beautiful island, Amanda finds herself caught up in a murder mystery in which no one, not even the attractive painter Steven Howard, is quite what they seem . . .

☐ *Lace* **Shirley Conran**

Lace is, quite simply, a publishing sensation: the story of Judy, Kate, Pagan and Maxine; the bestselling novel that teaches men about women, and women about themselves. 'Riches, bitches, sex and jetsetters' locations – they're all there' – *Sunday Express*

A CHOICE OF PENGUINS

☐ *West of Sunset* **Dirk Bogarde**

'His virtues as a writer are precisely those which make him the most compelling screen actor of his generation,' is what *The Times* said about Bogarde's savage, funny, romantic novel set in the gaudy wastes of Los Angeles.

☐ *The Riverside Villas Murder* **Kingsley Amis**

Marital duplicity, sexual discovery and murder with a thirties backcloth: 'Amis in top form' – *The Times*. 'Delectable from page to page . . . effortlessly witty' – C. P. Snow in the *Financial Times*

☐ *A Dark and Distant Shore* **Reay Tannahill**

Vilia is the unforgettable heroine. Kinveil Castle is her destiny, in this full-blooded saga spanning a century of Victoriana, empire, hatreds and love affairs. 'A marvellous blend of *Gone with the Wind* and *The Thorn Birds*. You will enjoy every page' – *Daily Mirror*

☐ *Kingsley's Touch* **John Collee**

'Gripping . . . I recommend this chilling and elegantly written medical thriller' – *Daily Express*. 'An absolutely outstanding storyteller' – *Daily Telegraph*

☐ *The Far Pavilions* **M. M. Kaye**

Holding all the romance and high adventure of nineteenth-century India, M. M. Kaye's magnificent, now famous, novel has at its heart the passionate love of an Englishman for Juli, his Indian princess. 'Wildly exciting' – *Daily Telegraph*

A CHOICE OF PENGUINS

A CHOICE OF PENGUINS

☐ *Man and the Natural World* **Keith Thomas**

Changing attitudes in England, 1500–1800. 'An encyclopedic study of man's relationship to animals and plants . . . a book to read again and again' – Paul Theroux, *Sunday Times* Books of the Year

☐ *Jean Rhys: Letters 1931–66*
Edited by Francis Wyndham and Diana Melly

'Eloquent and invaluable . . . her life emerges, and with it a portrait of an unexpectedly indomitable figure' – Marina Warner in the *Sunday Times*

☐ *The French Revolution* **Christopher Hibbert**

'One of the best accounts of the Revolution that I know . . . Mr Hibbert is outstanding' – J. H. Plumb in the *Sunday Telegraph*

☐ *Isak Dinesen* **Judith Thurman**

The acclaimed life of Karen Blixen, 'beautiful bride, disappointed wife, radiant lover, bereft and widowed woman, writer, sibyl, Scheherazade, child of Lucifer, Baroness; always a unique human being . . . an assiduously researched and finely narrated biography' – *Books & Bookmen*

☐ *The Amateur Naturalist*
Gerald Durrell with Lee Durrell

'Delight . . . on every page . . . packed with authoritative writing, learning without pomposity . . . it represents a real bargain' – *The Times Educational Supplement.* 'What treats are in store for the average British household' – *Daily Express*

☐ *When the Wind Blows* **Raymond Briggs**

'A visual parable against nuclear war: all the more chilling for being in the form of a strip cartoon' – *Sunday Times.* 'The most eloquent anti-Bomb statement you are likely to read' – *Daily Mail*

A CHOICE OF PENGUINS

☐ *Small World* **David Lodge**

A jet-propelled academic romance, sequel to *Changing Places*. 'A new comic débâcle on every page' – *The Times*. 'Here is everything one expects from Lodge but three times as entertaining as anything he has written before' – *Sunday Telegraph*

☐ *The Neverending Story* **Michael Ende**

The international bestseller, now a major film: 'A tale of magical adventure, pursuit and delay, danger, suspense, triumph' – *The Times Literary Supplement*

☐ *The Sword of Honour Trilogy* **Evelyn Waugh**

Containing *Men at Arms, Officers and Gentlemen* and *Unconditional Surrender*, the trilogy described by Cyril Connolly as 'unquestionably the finest novels to have come out of the war'.

☐ *The Honorary Consul* **Graham Greene**

In a provincial Argentinian town, a group of revolutionaries kidnap the wrong man . . . 'The tension never relaxes and one reads hungrily from page to page, dreading the moment it will all end' – Auberon Waugh in the *Evening Standard*

☐ *The First Rumpole Omnibus* **John Mortimer**

Containing *Rumpole of the Bailey, The Trials of Rumpole* and *Rumpole's Return*. 'A fruity, foxy masterpiece, defender of our wilting faith in mankind' – *Sunday Times*

☐ *Scandal* **A. N. Wilson**

Sexual peccadillos, treason and blackmail are all ingredients on the boil in A. N. Wilson's new, *cordon noir* comedy. 'Drily witty, deliciously nasty' – *Sunday Telegraph*

A CHOICE OF PENGUINS

☐ *Stanley and the Women* **Kingsley Amis**

'Very good, very powerful . . . beautifully written . . . This is Amis *père* at his best' – Anthony Burgess in the *Observer*. 'Everybody should read it' – *Daily Mail*

☐ *The Mysterious Mr Ripley* **Patricia Highsmith**

Containing *The Talented Mr Ripley*, *Ripley Underground* and *Ripley's Game*. 'Patricia Highsmith is the poet of apprehension' – Graham Greene. 'The Ripley books are marvellously, insanely readable' – *The Times*

☐ *Earthly Powers* **Anthony Burgess**

'Crowded, crammed, bursting with manic erudition, garlicky puns, omnilingual jokes . . . (a novel) which meshes the real and personalized history of the twentieth century' – Martin Amis

☐ *Life & Times of Michael K* **J. M. Coetzee**

The Booker Prize-winning novel: 'It is hard to convey . . . just what Coetzee's special quality is. His writing gives off whiffs of Conrad, of Nabokov, of Golding, of the Paul Theroux of *The Mosquito Coast*. But he is none of these, he is a harsh, compelling new voice' – Victoria Glendinning

☐ *The Stories of William Trevor*

'Trevor packs into each separate five or six thousand words more richness, more laughter, more ache, more multifarious human-ness than many good writers manage to get into a whole novel' – *Punch*

☐ *The Book of Laughter and Forgetting*
   Milan Kundera

'A whirling dance of a book . . . a masterpiece full of angels, terror, ostriches and love . . . No question about it. The most important novel published in Britain this year' – Salman Rushdie

A CHOICE OF PENGUINS

☐ ***The Diary of Virginia Woolf***
Edited by Quentin Bell and Anne Olivier Bell

'As an account of the intellectual and cultural life of our century, Virginia Woolf's diaries are invaluable; as the record of one bruised and unquiet mind, they are unique' – Peter Ackroyd in the *Sunday Times*

☐ Volume One
☐ Volume Two
☐ Volume Three
☐ Volume Four
☐ Volume Five

These books should be available at all good bookshops or newsagents, but if you live in the UK or the Republic of Ireland and have difficulty in getting to a bookshop, they can be ordered by post. Please indicate the titles required and fill in the form below.

NAME _____ BLOCK CAPITALS

ADDRESS _____

_____

_____

Enclose a cheque or postal order payable to The Penguin Bookshop to cover the total price of books ordered, plus 50p for postage. Readers in the Republic of Ireland should send £IR equivalent to the sterling prices, plus 67p for postage. Send to: The Penguin Bookshop, 54/56 Bridlesmith Gate, Nottingham, NG1 2GP.

You can also order by phoning (0602) 599295, and quoting your Barclaycard or Access number.

Every effort is made to ensure the accuracy of the price and availability of books at the time of going to press, but it is sometimes necessary to increase prices and in these circumstances retail prices may be shown on the covers of books which may differ from the prices shown in this list or elsewhere. This list is not an offer to supply any book.

This order service is only available to residents in the UK and the Republic of Ireland.

● ● ●